विघ्नेश्वराय नमः

Devotion & Divinity

GORTI VISWESWARA RAO

INDIA • SINGAPORE • MALAYSIA

ISBN 979-8-89233-981-0

Dedication

I dedicate this small volume to my (late) parents who bestowed on me this body, mind and intellect so that I am able to conveniently and fully offer prayers to HIM and remember HIM constantly.

An invocation - Gayatri maha mantra japa (sloka in Sanskrit)

ॐ भूर्भुवः स्वः तत्सवितुर्वरेण्यं

भर्गो देवस्य धीमहि धियो यो नः प्रचोदयात्

(*Sloka* in *Rig Veda*, 3rd mandala*)

Meaning of the *sloka* (verse)

I invoke the creator, the Supreme God almighty, who kindles all beings in this physical world and request HIM to illumine my intellect.

* *mandala* means book

Prayer to Devi Saraswati

सरस्वति नमस्तुभ्यं वरदे कामरूपिणि।

विद्यारम्भं करिष्यामि सिद्धिर्भवतु मे सदा॥

(*sloka* in *Sanskrit*)

Meaning of the verse:

Salutations to *Devi Saraswati*, the Goddess, who is the giver of boons and fulfiller of wishes; O *Devi*, when I begin my studies, please bestow on me always the capacity of right understanding.

Author's Self-Introduction

While I feel inappropriate to acquaint myself with the readers, I treat this requirement of penning my own introduction as HIS (*Paramaatma*'s) directive and write the following few words about myself:

Place of birth:

Amalapuram, East Godavari district, Andhra Pradesh, India.

Date of birth:

20th August 1947

Education:

BSc.: 1965. SKBR College, Amalapuram, East Godavari district, Andhra Pradesh, India.

BE: 1968. Government College of Engineering, Kakinada, East Godavari district, Andhra Pradesh, India

PhD: 1989. Indian Institute of Science, Bangalore, India

Books:

Coauthored a couple of engineering books with a Professor friend, Debasish Roy, Indian Institute of Science, Bangalore, India

Present interests:

i) Trying to engage myself in HIS thoughts whenever and wherever it is possible

ii) giving guest lectures on my subject of education, of course, with constant remembrance in mind of the *sloka* (hymn or verse) of *Adi Sankaracharya*[1] - *Bhaja Govindam Bhaja Govindam, Govindam Bhaja moodha mathe...*[2]

1 *Adi Sankaracharya [509 BC-477 BC]* - a marvellous personality with a short life span of 32 years; A spiritual *guru* (teacher) and considered to be God's incarnate; Advocated *advaitic* philosophy (non-dualism) - a unified universal view of *Vedanta*, that is: identity of the self with the super self or *Paramaatma*; Recognized for his illustrious works, *bhashyas* (commentaries) on ancient Indian texts and poetry (*stotras*); To name a few, his *bhashyas*/commentaries on ten main *Upanishads* and *Bhagavad Gita* are well-known

2 a part of a hymn scripted by *Adi Sankaracharya* in one of his eminent compositions (in Sanskrit) called '*Bhajagovindam*'; Addressing an elderly old person who is found struggling to learn Sanskrit grammar, *Adi Sankaracharya* says in the hymn implying a rebuke, 'Oh ignorant soul! worship *Govinda*, worship *Govinda*, Rules of grammar won't save you at the time of your death, worship Govinda'; Here note that *Govinda* is another name to Sri Krishna., the incarnate of *Paramaatma*

Contents

Acknowledgements

I humbly acknowledge the benevolent Almighty for the inspiration infused in me throughout the writing of this volume on 'Devotion (on HIM) and (HIS) Divinity'.

(Visweswara Rao Gorti)

The Prelude

[3]Hare Rama Hare Rama
Rama Rama Hare Hare
Hare Krishna Hare Krishna
Krishna Krishna Hare Hare

The above enchanting rhyme is the inspiration behind my attempt to write this book. However, I am initially in a wavering state to decide whether the book what I attempt to write is intended for persons of youth or old people like me. The reason is that I selected a subject which speaks about the sole essence of this human life as elucidated in the following *sloka* of Bhagavad Gita:

पुरुषः स परः पार्थ भक्त्या लभ्यस्त्वनन्यया।
यस्यान्तःस्थानि भूतानि येन सर्वमिदं ततम्॥ 8.22 ॥

(Meaning of the verse – It is the *ananya bhakti* (undivided and unflinching **devotion**) – that alone leads one to **divinity** and the omnipresent *Paramaatma*)

3 Chanting of this rhyme is initiated by *Chaitanya Mahaprabhu* [1485 – 1533] – a spiritual leader who advocated *Bhakti yoga* and taught that pure devotion is the principal way to attain liberation. Propagation of this rhyme all over the world is solely achieved because of the devotees/followers of ISKCON (International School of Krishna CONsciousness) which is founded by *Chaitanya Mahaprabhu*

Thus, my first thought to write a book on such awe-inspiring theme '*devotion* and *divinity*' to particularly attract young minds to read and rejoice has led me to a pensive mood. Yet, my immediate reaction is not to give way to such a wistful thinking but to divert the energy to make it plausible. It may require a good effort to amalgamate the two themes in such a fashion to kindle enough interest in the youthful minds also. In young age, our parents are everything for us and they are the Gods and we are devoted to them. We have absolute faith in them and depend on them fully and they take care of us in an absolute sense. *Paramaatma* also says in the following *sloka* of Bhagavad Gita:

अनन्याश्चिन्तयन्तो मां ये जनाः पर्युपासते।
एषां नित्याभियुक्तानां योगक्षेमं वहाम्यहम्॥ 9.22 ॥

(Meaning of the verse – whoever worships ME with *ananya bhakti* (unwavering devotion) and fully depends on ME is taken care of by ME)

Devotion

Devotion towards any person/persons fills our heart with love and affection. It may also lead to total surrender. A theist (believer in the Supreme Almighty) is one such being. Here, one may entertain a doubt if such a state of devotion and surrender is beneficial. It may also raise a question whether, with dependency, it may weaken a person physically and mentally. This is only an unfounded misgiving or suspicion. For instance, as we grow in age, our dependency on our parents generally reduces and in fact, they themselves suggest to us to be independent. One needs to be more circumspect when he makes a comparison of this situation in our mortal life with the divine thought of surrendering ourselves to the God Almighty. Here, one must infer a true understanding of oneself from the messages/advices given by *Bhagavwaan* Sri Krishna in *Bhagavad Gita*. Indeed, each and every *sloka* indicates the right way of life that one needs to follow, in general, for fulfilment of this birth as a human being. It encourages us to properly channelize our way of thinking to tackle every trivial or major issue that may arise and bother us in this mundane life due to *prarabdha karma*[4].

Dependency always exists in one's life in this birth. One may feel that he has become, at one stage, independent of parents' care but in fact at every other stage needs to depend on one or the other for his progress in life. He depends on his gurus (teachers) to receive knowledge from them and on his superiors for his further advancement in his professional career. Even coming to the trivial matter of a travel in air, he depends on the pilot for his safety and when he needs to cross a river, dependency on the boatman's skill in rowing the boat is apparent. This is the panoramic or all-inclusive view of every one's life in this birth. On the other hand, what is advocated in Gita is simple: we have this life in human form which may be transitory and impermanent, yet it is difficult to get and it is imminent that one needs to properly channelize his activities onto the path of *saatvic tapas*[5] (contained in *slokas* 14-17 in Chapter 17 of Bhagavad Gita:

4 action (good or bad) accrued from previous births

5 *Saatvic* quality is one of goodness, accommodating, forgiveness and nobility; *tapas* means *puja* or worship

देवद्विजगुरुप्राज्ञपूजनं शौचमार्जवम्
ब्रह्मचर्यमहिंसा च शारीरं तप
उच्यते॥17-14॥

अनुद्वेगकरं वाक्यं सत्यं प्रियहितं
च यत्।
स्वाध्यायाभ्यसनं चैव वाङ्मयं तप
उच्यते॥17-15॥

मनः प्रसादः सौम्यत्वं
मौनमात्मविनिग्रहः
भावसंशुद्धिरित्येतत्तपो
मानसमुच्यते॥17-16॥

श्रद्धया परया तप्तं तपस्तत्त्रिविधं
नरैः
अफलाकाङ्क्षिभिर्युक्तैः सात्त्विकं
परिचक्षते॥17-17॥

Essential meaning of the above *slokas*: Bhagawaan describes *saatvic tapas* as performing actions by body, speech and thought without an expectation on their result, i.e., worshipping *Paramaatma* and *gurus* (teachers), maintaining purity, honesty, serenity, and no-violent, truthful and helpful attitude, keeping mental peace and control.

From a commoner's point of view, that is, from the viewpoint of a person leading a mundane life, the simple way is to follow a *saatvic* mode of living, particularly in being equanimous and holding goodwill towards all, trying to keep calm and composed in all situations and getting engaged in dutiful activities with scant regard on their result. Here, one must pay heed to the specific advice given in the last verse of *Sadhana Panchakam*[6] by *Sri Adi Sankaracharya* which is elucidated below:

"In solitude, live joyously. Quieten your mind in the Supreme Lord, Realise and see the All-pervading Self everywhere. Recognise that the finite universe is a projection of the Self.

---

6 Sadhana means practice and *Panchakam* means five verses or *slokas*. In this singular composition, Adi Sankaracharya enumerates step-by-step practice required by a mortal to lead a spiritual way of life that finally leads him to the state of Divine realization.

Conquer the effects of the deeds done in earlier lives by the present right action. Through wisdom, become detached from future actions, experience and exhaust "prarabdha", the fruits of past actions. Thereafter, live absorbed in the thought – "I am Brahman"!".

In a transcendental stage, devotion towards the Creator of this world makes one understand that he is not different from HIM. Faith in HIM brings one close to HIM. We are fortunate enough to know in our present times also, devotees of this genre. *Annamaya*[7], *Sant Tulasi das*[8], *Bhakta Ramdasu*[9] are such devotees who dedicated their lives solely in amalgamating themselves with HIM and singing in praise of HIM till their last breath. In mundane terms, a doctor showing devotion towards his profession develops self-confidence and faith in his skills in offering a healing touch to the needy and this selfless service of his is indeed divine. Let us understand that devotion leads to faith and faith is divinity.

---

7 Annamaya [1408-1503] – Mystical poet known for his devotional songs in 'Telugu' language in praise of Lord Sri Venkateswara (*Paramaatma* incarnate), TTD, Andhra Pradesh, India

8 Sant Tulasi das [1532-1623] - Hindu saint and poet, renowned for his devotion to the deity Sri Ram (an incarnation of *Paramaatma*). Popular for his '*dohe*', a form of self-contained rhyming couplets in poetry; His life is an example to know that *Paramaatma* is attainable through pure bhakti

9 *Bhadrachala Ramdasu* [1620-1688]– a saint poet of Sri Rama popularly known for his devotional songs written in Telugu language and revered for the great bhakti content in these songs

Divinity

Divinity is inherently and naturally present in everybody. It is not anything that is a strange or unintelligible matter and nor a thing that is not discernible. One only needs to recognize this quality within oneself and practice for *self-realization*[10]. A virtuous quality in a person is itself divinity or Godly. For instance, qualities like charity and service to needy, purity within and without, an attitude of sacrifice, kindness towards all, softness in speech or actions, forgiveness, enmity towards none and humility or self-consciousness in receiving praise are divine. This is exactly the core message given by Bhagawaan Sri Krishna in *slokas* 1-3, Chapter 16, *Bhagavad Gita*.

अभयं सत्त्वसंशुद्धिर्ज्ञानयोगव्यवस्थितिः।
दानं दमश्च यज्ञश्च स्वाध्यायस्तप आर्जवम्॥16-1॥

अहिंसा सत्यमक्रोधस्त्यागः शान्तिरपैशुनम्।
दया भूतेष्वलोलुप्त्वं मार्दवं ह्रीरचापलम्॥16-2॥

तेजः क्षमा धृतिः शौचमद्रोहो नातिमानिता।
भवन्ति संपदं दैवीमभिजातस्य भारत॥16-3॥

One possessing these divine qualities is fearless and free of ego and is an accomplished person. One can look at such a person as a living form of GOD almighty. In our *Kaliyuga* or the present age, we had such illustrious personalities, philosophers, and selfless

10 As a first step to self-realization, Sri Ramana Maharshi (see footnote 11 below) always insisted his devotees to question themselves 'who am I?' and urged them to ' know thyself '. One should get into a self-introspection mode and confront oneself with 'why I am here? and 'what is the purpose of this life? Through this persistent self-enquiry only, it is possible to recognize one's true self and identity with the divine, all-pervading, and Omni-present *Paramaatma*

persons like *Sri Ramana Mahirshi*[11], *Chaitanya Mahaprabhu, Sri Chandrasekhara Saraswati Paramcharya*[12] of *Kanchi Kaamakoti, Sri Ramakrishna Paramahamsa*[13], *Swami Vivekananda*[14], *Mother Teresa*[15] who with a message of universal oneness and self-less service so profoundly served the mankind that they must be HIS *vibhutis* (incarnations).

11 Sri Ramana Maharshi [1879-1950]– One of the greatest spiritual sages; Revered for his teaching of self-inquiry in the form of the divine message 'know thyself '; Worshipped by all for his direct teaching through silence

12 Sri Chandrasekharendra Saraswati of Kanchi Kaamakoti [1884 - 1994] – A great sage and philosopher; Was a religious head of the Kanchi_Kamakoti_Peetham; Practiced the Advaita philosophy expounded by Adi Shankaracharya; Propagated the message "develop unshakeable faith in God and tolerance to wipe out sorrows"

13 Sri Ramakrishna Paramahamsa [1836 - 1886]- A great philosopher, a mystic and a yogi; Propagated the message that the ultimate goal of every living soul is God-realization and all religions are different routes that lead up to a single goal, that is God

14 Swami Vivekananda [1863-1902] – Original name is Narendranath Datta; Disciple of Sri Ramakrishna Paramahamsa; Addressed the parliament of the World's Religions in Chicago in 1893 and familiarized the western world with *Vedanta* philosophy and *yoga*

15 Mother Teresa [1910 – 1997] - She is an Albenian; founded the Missionaries of Charity in 1950; Revered by many for her charitable work and wholehearted free service to the poorest of the poor which is nothing but *bhuta daya* (compassion towards all) and the service requires immense patience (*kshama*); these two qualities are virtues that *Paramaatma* professed for mankind to cultivate (Chapter 16, Verses 2-3) as a means to self-realization

Devotees and the Divine – Ramayana (of Valmiki[16])

In the times of *Treta yuga*[17], Anjaneya[18] and Sri Rama[19] respectively symbolize a devout devotee and a Divine personality. From *Valmiki Ramayana*[20] we all became familiar with the historical events that surrounded the life of *Sri Rama* and his spouse *Sita. Sri Rama*, even though he is a God's incarnation and has taken birth as a human, solely to annihilate the wicked *asura*[21] king *Ravana*[22],

---

16 *Valmiki* is the sage who wrote *Ramayana* and is known as *adi kavi* (first poet) with *Ramayana* being the first epic. *Valmiki* was known by birth as *Agni Sarma;* During his period of *tapas* (meditation) for long years, he got fully covered by anthills and so much so got the name of *Valmiki;* Sighting the pitiable killing of one of the crane couple involved in mating, by a hunter, the first *Sanskrit sloka* (verse) came out of him as a rebuke on the hunter:

मा निषाद प्रतिष्ठां त्वमगमः शाश्वतीः समाः। यत्क्रौञ्चमिथुनादेकमवधीः काममोहितम्॥	<u>Meaning of the verse:</u> You will find no rest for the long years of Eternity, for you killed a bird in love and unsuspecting

17 In *yuga* cycle as counted in India, the *Treta Yuga* is the second of the four *yugas* and spans 1,296,000 solar years where one solar year is the familiar calendar year which is approximately equal to 365.25 days

18 Anjaneya is the son of the wind God and chief among the *vanaras* (see also foot note 26)

19 Sri Rama is a an incarnate of *Vishnu* God and is an *avatara* (appearance) in human form in *Treta yuga*; He is born to *Kausalya*, wife of *Dasaratha*, the king of *Ayodhya*; *Ayodhya is presently a city in Uttara Pradesh, India;* It is located near the river *Sarayu.*

20 *Ramayana* was written in *Sanskrit* by *Maharshi Valmiki*

21 Meaning a demon; *asura* is a sanskrit word also termed as a '*rakshasa*'; one may understand '*asura*' as a person with demoniac qualities

22 *Ravana* is the king of *asuras* (demons); He is born to the great sage *Vishrava*, and his wife *Kaikesi* in *Treta yuga*. He is known to be a great worshipper of Shiva (God incarnate); A story goes that he is said to be one of the two guards (*Jaya* and *Vijaya*) at the *Vaikuntham* (the dwelling place of *Vishnu*,

never indicated his divine identifications himself. He showed his emotions at every stage of his life in the same way, humans exhibit. He grieved over the death of King *Dasaratha*, his father, wailed and showed his *krodha* (anger) over the abduction of *Sita* by *Ravana*. However, we are amply made to know his divine qualities by *Maharshi Viswamitra*[23] who had taken the two young brothers *Rama* and *Lakshmana* with him on the holy errand of protecting his *ashram* (abode) known as *Siddhaashram* from the wanton attacks by *asuras*. The incidents involving *Ahalya*[24] and *Shabari*[25] also confirm this belief.

---

the *Paramaatma*). To their bad luck, one day a curse befell on them from four sages (*Sanandana, Sanaka, Sanat Sujata and Sanat Kumara*), when the latter were prevented from entering the Sanctum Sanctorum of *Vishnu*. He was given a choice by *Vishnu* whether they wish to be away from him for many births as a friend or to be away from HIM for only few births but as a foe. they opted for the second one since it was only few births they would be away from their Lord. Thus, they took birth in *Treta yuga* as Ravana and *Kumbhakarna*. Thus, in *Treta yuga*, Ravana abducted *Sita*, wife of Sri Rama and became the meanest foe and met his death in the hands of Sri Rama; *Kumbhakarna* also met the same fate.

23 *Maharshi Viswamitra* was a king by birth; At one time in his life he had a duel with *Maharshi Vasishta* in respect of attaining the highest position of a *Maharshi*. He renounced the royal status and achieved his goal by doing a rigorous *tapas* for thousands of years and after meeting failures in between. The great *Maharshi Viswamitra* is greatly credited for his composition of *Gayatri mantra* (Page ii???)

24 Wife of the sage *Gautama Maharishi*. It is said (*Bala Kanda, Ramayana*) that she was seduced by *Indra* (the king of heaven), cursed by her husband for infidelity and was liberated from the curse by *Sri Rama* on the advice of *Maharshi Viswamitra*

25 Originally a village woman; She served the sage *Matanga* for many years; The sage, at the time of his demise, blessed her that she would get an opportunity to meet Sri Rama in her life. With utmost devotion, she waited for the event to happen which got fulfilled when *Sri Rama* with sage *Viswamitra* visited her ashram. Rama accepted the sweet berries given by her even after she told him

Sabari offering berries to Sri Rama and Lakshmana after tasting them to check their sweetness – that is a pinnacle of devotion!

---

with fondness that she tasted them beforehand to check their sweetness. To Lakshmana's query, Sri Rama said, "whosoever offers a fruit, a leaf, a flower or water with love and affection, I take it with great joy". One finds the same message in *sloka* 26, Chapter 9, Bhagavad Gita:

पत्रं पुष्पं फलं तोयं यो मे भक्त्या प्रयच्छति। तदहं भक्त्युपहृतमश्नामि प्रयतात्मनः॥	Meaning of the verse: Whosoever offers HIM with devotion and a pure mind, a leaf, a flower, a fruit or a little water - HE accepts it

How Anjaneya also recognized the divinity in *Sri Rama* and how he, as a mighty *vanara*[26], played an important role in serving his divine master all through the critical times is well-known. Anjaneya is a close associate of the *vanara* king, Sugreeva[27] in the kingdom of *Kishkindha*[28].

It is Anjaneya who brought the two young princes *Rama* and *Lakshmana* and *vanara* king Sugreeva into a strong fold of friendship when the latter was indeed taking refuge in *Rishyamuka*[29] mountains out of fear for his life from his own brother Vali[30]. *Kishkindha kanda* describing the forging of friendship between Sugreeva and *Rama*

---

26 Forest dwelling people depicted in the epic *Ramayana* (of *Treta yuga*) as having the characteristics of monkeys; Described to be possessing supernatural abilities and purported to be created to help Sri Rama (God incarnate) in defeating the *asura* (demon) king *Ravana*.

27 Sugreeva is the younger brother of Vali who ruled *Kishkindha* (see foot note 30 below). To his misfortune, there had arisen a strong misunderstanding between the two brothers that made Sugreeva to run away in fear of his brother and took refuge in *Rishyamuka* mountains where Vali could not enter because of the curse by the sage *Mathanga*; Sugreeva is said to be the son of sun deity

28 It is the kingdom of *vanaras* and is ruled by Sugreeva after the death of his brother Vali. In *Treta yuga*, this kingdom is situated in *Dandaka* forest in *Vindhya* mountain range.

29 Is a mountain region habituated by the sage *Mathanga* in *Treta yuga*; The mountain is on other side of the Hampi city, crossing the Tungabhadra River in Karnataka state, India

30 Vali is the king of *vanaras* ruling *Kishkindha* in the times of *Treta yuga*; He is the elder brother of Sugreeva; It is said that nobody can stand a battle with him due to a boon that any opponent facing him loses half of his strength. *Rama* killed him with an arrow standing behind a tree; When questioned by Vali why he killed him anonymously, Rama answered that as a prince of *Ayodhya*, he has the right to punish evil persons and Vali wronged Sugreeva who is younger to him and is to be forgiven for his mistakes

and the incidents that quickly followed is central to the whole *Ramayana*.

It is really astounding to see the arrival of trillions of *vanaras* at the strong behest of Sugreeva from all over the nook and corner of the earth and their pursuit in the four directions in search of *Sita* and her abductor *Ravana*. We will be definitely overwhelmed to see Anjaneya in *Sundara kanda*[31] describing to *Sita* the immeasurable strength of these warrior *vanaras* as: *Surrounded by millions of monkeys, that destroyer of titans (*Sugreeva*) will come hither without delay. There are, under his command, monkeys endowed with valour, energy and extreme prowess, swift as thought, able to go upward or downward and to every side, nothing can impede their course, no task, however hard, defeats their immeasurable courage. Nay, more than once, by their amazing endurance, they have encircled the entire earth with its seas and mountains on every side, by resorting to the wind's path".*

---

31 *Sundara Kanda* is the fifth chapter in *Ramayana*; It depicts the valour and pure devotion of Anjaneya towards Rama; The verse below the beauty of the whole *Sundara kanda*:

सुन्दरे सुन्दरो रामः सुन्दरे सुन्दरी कथा सुन्दरे सुन्दरी सीता सुन्दरे सुन्दरं वनम्। सुन्दरे सुन्दरं काव्यं सुन्दरे सुन्दरः कपिः सुन्दरे सुन्दरं मन्त्रं सुन्दरे किं न सुन्दरम्॥
<u>Meaning of the verse:</u> Sri Rama is beautiful and so is his story, Mother Sita is not just beautiful by appearance but also most beautiful by her deeds. The Ashoka Vanam of Lanka as described in Sundara *kanda* by Valmiki is beautiful and enchanting with many trees, lakes and birds. This also includes the beauty of the entire narration of this Kanda in the form of poems. It also depicts the beauty of the Kapi (*vanara* or monkey), i.e Anjaneya. It signifies that every aspect in Sundara Kanda is just nothing but beautiful

In a sequel to this incidence, we find Anjaneya describing their infinite strength to the *asuras* in *Lanka*[32] during his fight with them as: *some are as strong as elephants, others ten times as strong, some have the energy of a thousand elephants, some of a whole herd and some have the strength of the wind, while a few possess a strength that may not be measured. Such are the monkeys, armed with teeth and claws, that in hundreds and thousands and millions, will accompany* Sugreeva *when he comes to exterminate you all".*

In an answer to Rama's query - *How is it that thou knowest all the quarters of the earth ?* - it is a wonder to hear Sugreeva replying that in an attempt to escape from wicked Vali pursuing him everywhere, he traversed endlessly and grew conversant with every kind of region on earth ([33]*sargas* 40-47, *Kishkindha kanda, Valmiki Ramayana*).

32 Region reigned by *asura* king, *Ravana*

33 Sugreeva's knowledge of physical world is acquired when Vali put him to flight. Rama enquires with Sugreeva as to how Sugreeva has many details of lands, countries, rivers, and mountains. In reply, Sugreeva says that when repulsed by Vali he was on the run to pillar to post, until he finally settled on Mt. Rishyamuka. During such a plighted flight, Sugreeva says, he acquired a direct and personal knowledge of earth. Sugreeva explains the topography and geography of Eastern side of the *jambuu dweepa*, 'the Indian subcontinent,' and its eastward, comprising whole of South-East Asia. This is the first chronicle ever recorded about the lands and oceans, islands and dwellers in there, as far as Ancient Indian Geography is concerned. Sugreeva gives a vivid picture of the southern side of *Jambu dweepa* up to the south-most part of passable regions. Sugreeva sends troops to west side to search for Seetha under the leadership of Sushena, the father of lady Tara. Describing the various and magnificent mountains that are situated at the northwest of India, and also the ocean down south to it, namely the present Arabian Sea and almost up to Persian provinces, he orders monkey troops to return within one month's time. Sugreeva sends troops to north with a valorous *vanara* named Shatabali as the chief in search of Seetha. He gives an account of the snowy regions and provinces of northern side and asks them to search in the places of Yavana, Kuru, and Darads etc., civilisations. Sugreeva specially

His description that *earth appeared to him like the reflection of a whirling firebrand seen in a mirror or a puddle* makes us awe-struck with the truth contained in his statement.

In the midst of this discussion on 'Devotees and the Divine - *Ramayana*', I have a reason in penning this short description of the *vanara* army. When I think of these faithful and valiant *vanaras,* my mind is filled with an unknown kind of joy in imagining their *devotion* to their duty and their master. In these multitude of births and deaths of a *jivaatma, what if I were also a small vanara yodha* (warrior) in *Treta yuga*? Every time when I read *Sundara kanda* and I read the particular *slokas* (in sarga 1) mentioning about the giant leap of Anjaneya over the mighty ocean and on the way to *Lanka,* the abode of *asura* king *Ravana,* I always go into a trance and conjure up a vision of myself being a tiny sand particle clinging to the body of Anjaneya and circumambulating along with him in *Lanka* and returning back to *Kishkindha*. So, how much of a fortune I must have, to be born even as a small *vanara* moving with them in those times?

---

informs them about a divine province called Uttara Kuru and a heavenly mountain called Mt. Soma on which Brahma, Vishnu and Shiva make sojourn for its sacredness

Sugreeva and the army of vanaras

Let it be a factual happening and not a dream. The name I give myself is Achala in first part of this book.

Devotees and the Divine – Maha Bhagavatam (of Veda Vyasa[34] and Pothana[35])

In *Dwapur yuga*[36], all the mankind was so fortunate that all were blessed to have *Paramaatma* born amongst them with the name

Vasudeva and Devaki having darshan of Sri Maha Vishnu;
Sri Krishna born in a prison cell

---

34 Sage Vyasa was the son of sage Parasara and Satyavati. He is also known as Veda Vyasa since he classified the Vedas and this categorization greatly helped in comprehending the divine knowledge contained in Vedas. He is credited to be an incarnation of Lord Vishnu and he wrote the epic Maha Bharata. He also features as an important character in it. Vyasa is also credited with the writing of the eighteen major puranas.

35 *Pothana* (1450–1510) – A saintly poet born in *Bammera* village, Telangana state, India; Known for his astounding devotion towards Sri Rama; Well-known for his scholarly translation by name *Sri Maha Bhagavatamu* written in Telugu language of *Veda Vyasa*'s *Srimad Bhagavatam* (originally in Sanskrit)

36 In *yuga* cycle as counted in India, the *Dwapur Yuga* is the third of the four *yugas* and spans *864,000 solar years* where one solar year is the familiar calendar year which is approximately equal to 365.25 days

Krishna[37] and grown along with them. HE[38] enchanted all in *Gokula*[39] even as a child with HIS divine prowess.

Krishna's is an *avatara* (incarnation) of *Paramaatma* that is said to be a *paripurnavatara* (an incarnation said to be complete). Its meaning signifies a complete material appearance in human form of the *nirguna*[40], *nirakara*[41], omniscient and omnipresent *Paramaatma*. HIS elder brother is *Balarama*[42] who also grew along with HIM. Krishna's birth has a solemn purpose. This we find in *sloka* 7, Chapter 4 of Bhagavad Gita:

---

37 Krishna is the Supreme Almighty. Unlike Rama in *Ramayana*, Krishna exhibited to the world from the instant of HIS birth that HE is the *Paramaatama* and HE is the protector and destructor of this world. HE appeared in HIS *chathurbhuja rupam* (see Figure above on this page) even at the time HIS birth itself to HIS parents. *Devaki*, the mother of Krishna, showed her innocent motherly concern and requested HIM to withdraw the supreme appearance so as to escape the attention of the sinner, *Kamsa*. Even though HE graced this earth in a human form, is it possible to fully describe the Supreme to our full satisfation? Our ignorant minds may try to imagine and conjure up an image that is in reality is formless. Better to bow down our heads in total surrender, close our eyes, wash HIS adorable feet with our tears of devotion and seek refuge in that *Purushothama*!

38 Since Krishna is understood and known to be Divinity personified by everybody, the words 'HE, HIS, HIM, HIMSELF will be used in this part of the book wherever the name is referred to.

39 Gokula is the place where Krishna has grown; It is around 10 Km to Madhura. Krishna was born in Madhura which is located in Uttar Pradesh and is about 50 Km away from Agra.

40 Devoid of qualities

41 Devoid of an appearance (formless)

42 While Krishna is regarded as an incarnation of *Vishnu, Balarama* is said to be an incarnation of Sesha, the serpent associated with Lord Vishnu, the God's incarnate

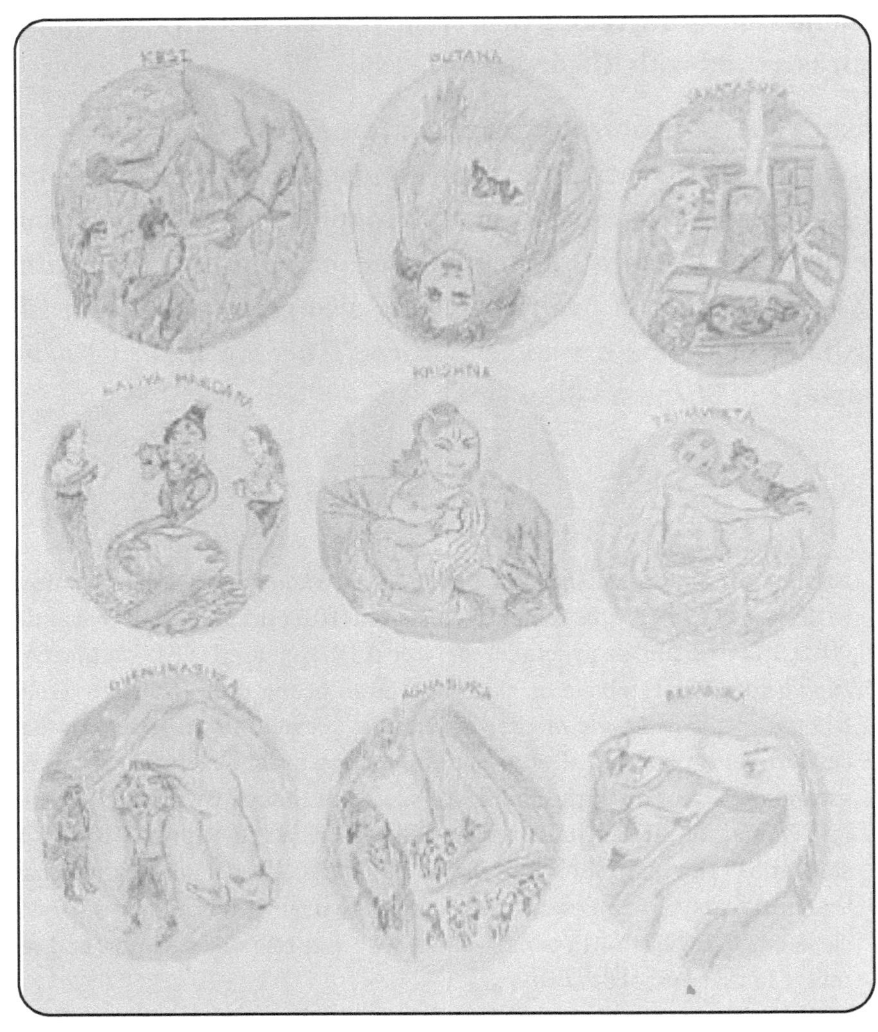

Asuras (demons) killed by Divine Krishna

यदा यदा हि धर्मस्य ग्लानिर्भवति भारत।
अभ्युत्थानमधर्मस्य तदात्मानं सृजाम्यहम्॥

(Meaning of the verse – O Bharata, whenever there is a weakening of dharma (morality) and rise of adharma (immorality), then I appear myself)

In *Dwapur yuga*, decline[43] of *dharma* rapidly started with people accustomed to *adharmic* (immoral) ways of living dominated by greed, anger and hatred. In consonance with *Paramaatma*'s declaration in the last *sloka*, HE incarnated in human form on this earth as Krishna in order to purge the society of these unworthy people. HIS incredible acts at the age of an young child, of killing the wicked *Putana* (demoness), *Shakaṭāsura* (cart demon), *Trinavarta* (whirlwind demon), *Vatsasura* (calf demon), *Bakasura*_(crane demon), *Aghasura* (snake demon), *Arishtasura* (bull demon), Kesi (horse demon), Vyomasura (bat demon) who are all sent by the evil king *Kamsa*[44] show HIS intentions.

HIS slaying later of *Kamsa, Sishupala and Dantvaktra*[45] all fall into the scheme of things devised by *Paramaatma*. Some in *Dwapur yuga* itself might not have realized the sublime reality behind HIS *avatara* as *Krishna*. This is in line with what Krishna says to Arjuna in in the following *sloka* in *Bhagavad Gita* (Chapter 9):

---

43 Here we need to interpret that declining is regarding the practice of *dharma*. With this in view, in the Kritha Yuga, it is said that it was on all four legs, and later in the Treta Yuga, dharma was only on three legs. Later in the Dwapur Yuga, it was only on two legs; and it is surmised that in the present Kali Yuga it stands only on one leg.

44 Kamsa was the king of Vrishni kingdom; He is the cousin brother of *Devaki*, the mother of Krishna; Learning through a prophecy that Krishna is his terminator, he made vain attempts to kill Krisna even when HE was an infant; Kamsa finally met his death in the hands of Krishna.

45 *Sishupala and Dantvaktra* were the same *Jaya* and *Vijaya*, the two guards at *Vaikuntham,* the dwelling place of Vishnu who faced the fate of separation from their Lord due to the curse from the four sages (*Sanandana, Sanaka, Sanat Sujata and Sanat Kumara)*. They took birth in *Dwapur yuga* and got killed by Krishna

अवजानन्ति मां मूढा मानुषीं तनुमाश्रितम्।
परं भावमजानन्तो मम भूतमहेश्वरम्॥ 9.11॥

(Meaning of the verse – when I assume human form in this mortal world, fools being unaware of MY higher nature as the Supreme Lord of all beings, disregard ME thinking that I am also commoner amongst them)

There are, however, many in *Gokula* who well realized the *Godly* effervescence in the little Krishna and felt it was fulfillment of their lives in being so near and dear to HIM. All the *gopala boys*[46] and girls who also grew along with Krishna are deeply devoted to HIM. They all partook in the childish chivalry exhibited by Krishna in playing mischievous pranks with all women folk in *Gokula* inviting their wrath at times which they exposed to Yasoda, the mother of Krishna. The joy derived by all in the end was sometimes marred by the strange incidents where Krishna had to punish the *asuras* sent by Kamsa from time to time. These happenings grieved Yasoda deeply and the motherly attitude to protect her son weighed more than her realization that HE is really the *Paramaatma* HIMSELF. We can imagine her plight – more astonishment and disbelief than delight - when HE, on being asked by her to open HIS mouth to see if HE had really eaten butter secretively, had exhibited the entire universe within HIS mouth. She was no doubt a blessed soul and what a glorious life it was to cajole and carry HIM in her hands, feed HIM with her milk, have HIM close to her chest, also innocently and ignorantly prod and nudge Krishna, the *Paramaatma*, now and then for HIS naughty behavior! Her pure devotion[47] had put her finally in the sacred role of a mother to the Supreme.

46 Cowherd boys

47 *See foot note 99*

The devotion in the hearts of all *gopikas*[48] grew into deep and unflinching faith in Krishna as they grew along with HIM in age. This is nothing strange as it is said[49] that the *gopikas* are indeed *rishis/*sages in their earlier birth who prayed *Paramaatma* and pleaded HIM for the boon that they be blessed with an opportunity to be near and dear to HIM and enjoy HIS bliss. Of course, they are *rishis* and *jnanis*[50] of yester *yugas* and it was definitely possible for them to do rigorous *tapas*[51] and achieve their priestly goals. In our present times, the same *devotion* and *faith* were shown by *Meera Bai, Chaitanya Mahaprabhu* and many other blessed souls and they all must have finally realized salvation and union with HIM.

We, commoners, with scant knowledge in *sastras* may be leading lives of commonplace in this *Kali yuga*. While this may be true, this shall not deter us in any way from developing devotion and faith in the Creator and the Ingenious Architect of this beautiful world. We need to be grateful to HIM in bestowing on us this life in human

---

48 *Gopikas* are ladies in *Gokula Brindavan* village where Krishna grew up and spent HIS youth under the care of HIS foster parents - Nanda and Yashoda. The *gopikas* had forsaken everything what they possessed in their lives and adored HIM with all their love. Their love is symbolic of *ananya* bhakti (profound devotion)

49 In Treta yuga, when Rama stays in Dandakaranya forest along with Sita (after he accepted banishment from Ayodhya), many sages were captivated by the beauty of Rama and wished to become women and get blessed with conjugal love with *Paramaatma*. Since Rama is an embodiment of Sanatana Dharma and an ideal king, the sages had his solemn benediction that *Paramaatma* descends again to the earth as Krishna in Dwapur yuga and their wish would be fulfilled when they also would have their birth as *gopikas* of Gokula and Brindavan. In this way they attained the perfection of spiritual life.

50 enlightened personalities

51 prayer with devotion

form and need to utilize it in *self-enquiry*[52] while going ahead with our duties whatever required at every stage and, to make it possible to engage ourselves in *Dhyana*[53] about the Invisible Supreme.

Having got engaged thus far in positive thinking about this mortal life, I have suddenly gone into a reverie and begun to visualize the possibility that I might have, after all, had a birth in *Dwapur yuga* also and spent a flowery life as a village belle in *Gokula* and moved in the close vicinity of the blessed devotees and Krishna, the Divine.

Let me make this dream a reality and give a name to myself as Achala in second part of the book.

Sri Krishna and *gopikas* of Brindavan

52 Through a practice of self-enquiry only, it is possible to recognize one's true self and identity with the divine and all-pervading and Omni-present *Paramaatma*. As Sri Ramana Maharshi always insisted his devotees to question themselves 'who am I?' and urged them to ' know thyself ' as a first step to self-realization, one shall get into a self-introspection mode and confront oneself with 'why I am here ? and 'what is the purpose of this life ?.

53 One can call it a *'maanasica tapas'*, i.e., prayer within the mind*;* As *Adi Sankaracharya* pronounced in *Maneesha Panchakam* that only by meditating with perfectly calm mind on HIM and not by any other extraordinary and special means, one can unify his intellect with the Bliss Supreme.

FIRST PART

Sri Rama, Sita Devi and Anjaneya

Hare Rama Hare Rama
Rama Rama Hare Hare

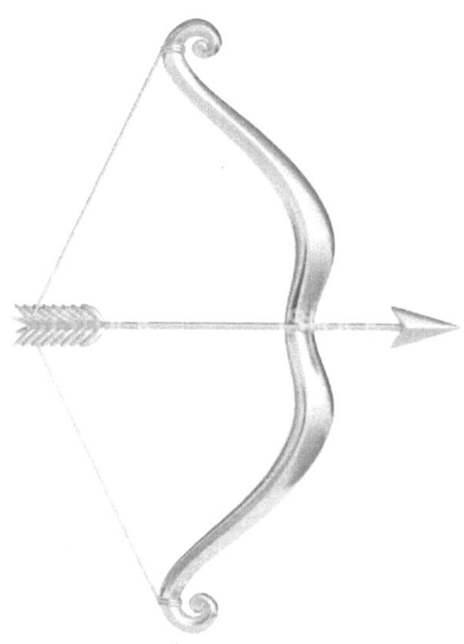

1.1 *Kishkindha kanda – Anjaneya, the devotee*

Of late, there is a stony silence in and around our place *Kishkindha*[54]. The reason is obvious. There is a frequent duel between our king Sugreeva and the reigning king Vali. We are presently living on *Rishyamuka* mountain. Our king Sugreeva is taking refuge here after being wrongly and cruelly exiled from the kingdom by his brother Vali. Even though our king is also a mighty combatant, he is unable to match Vali in each fight he has with the latter. The cause for the enmity between the two brothers is a *long story*[55] which I, as a young *vanara*, am ignorant of the details. My parents may be aware of the past but they did not share with me and I also had shown no interest in knowing it.

---

54 The kingdom of *Kishkindha* of *vanara* king Sugreeva is said to be a part of the *Dandaka aranya* (Dandaka forest*)* which stretched from the *Vindhiya* mountain range down to the south of India; Aranya means forest

55 Vali and Sugreeva are brothers and are fond of each other. Sugreeva served his brother faithfully when the latter was ruling *Kishkindha*. Their lives are peaceful till that fateful day when they chased their enemy by name *Mayavi* and roamed in the forest for long many years in search of their enemy. When Vali noticed *Mayavi* entering a cave, he asked his brother to keep a watch at the mouth of the cave till he returned. Vali went into the cave and Sugreeva waited near the cave with no traces of *Vali* returning even after a year. To his dismay, he noticed a stream of blood flowing out of the cave and heard the loud cries of *Mayavi*. He falsely supposed that Vali was killed by *Mayavi*. With a sorrowful mind, he returned to *Kishkindha* and also closed the mouth of the cave to prevent *Mayavi* from coming out. He subsequently assumed kingship on the advice of the ministreal *vanaras*. To his ill fate, Vali came out after killing *Mayavi* and was enraged when he found the cave closed. He easily came out of the cave and fully misunderstanding his brother's actions, he confronted his brother and banished him from the kingdom. Fearing Vali, Sugreeva ran away for his life and finally took refuge in the forest near *Rishyamuka* mountain. He was aware that Vali cannot tread into the area because of a curse from sage *Mathunga*.

I liked our dwelling place on the *Rishyamuka* mountain. It is beautiful and serene. It is full of young streams flowing over every place over the caves we live in. It is also inhabited by *rishis* (sages) who engage themselves in *tapas* and in *pujas* over *sacred fire*. In our childhood, myself and my friends used to visit the ashrams and play with the young lads who though humans showed interest and liked our company. They used to come with us to the forest after duly taking permission from their mothers. The mothers also liked us and often gave us fruits which we relished always.

So many years might have passed since and all of us are now part of Sugreeva's army. He made it compulsory for all grown-up male *vanaras* to join army at young age. We all went through lot of training in the beginning. In addition to acquiring combating skills like fist fighting and wrestling, it all includes lifting heavy boulders, uprooting trees of different sizes and throwing them for long distances and also attaining skills initially in running over trees and later flying freely without any support for many *yojanas*[56]. At least myself and some of my friends had the fortune of securing a place in the king's army even though it may be at a lower rung and a part of outer circle of *yodhas* (warriors).

56 unit of distance prevalent in ancient India; 1 yojana = about 8 miles = about 12.8 km

1.2 A meeting in Kishkindha of Anjaneya with the Divine Sri Rama and Lakshmana

In the last few days, I noticed and could sense a change in the mood of all of our people around Kishkindha. The reason I could understand and it is definitely due to the arrival of the two princes *Rama* and Lakshmana. Of course, I was also present on that day when Anjaneya brought them to our king Sugreeva. The first time I looked at them from a distance, I was attracted and also overwhelmed by their simplicity and at the same time some aura of their invincibility. I could also see the strange transformation in Anjaneya. My young mind also could decipher it as a powerful feeling of devotion and servitude that Anjaneya developed towards *Rama*, the elder prince. For me, Anjaneya is my idol. From my young age, I was fascinated by hearing about his many incredible *child-hood exploits*[57] from my father and about his superlative powers that he might have possessed. From the strange behavior in the last few days of my ideal hero and idol Anjaneya and the worshipping way he moved with the two princes, it looked for me as if he had finally found his

57 *child-hood exploits of* Anjaneya: As a child, Anjaneya rose to the skies to grab the sun. Assuming that the sun is a bright and delicious fruit, he wanted to eat it. *Indra*, the king of the heavens, was perplexed by the child's audacious act, he hit Anjaneya with his weapon called *Vajra*. That is the reason why Anjaneya's chin got lengthened a little and protruded forward and is also called *Hanuman*. Chin is called *hanu* in Sanskrit. The boy fell down unconscious with the blow by *Vajra*. *Vayu*, the celestial father of Anjaneya got annoyed and stopped his vital function of blowing. As this caused a sudden suffocation and trouble for breathing to all beings on earth, there was an urgency to appease *Vayu*. *Brahma*, the God incarnate and the creator of the whole universe showed his presence and showered blessings on the child that no weapon can hurt him and nor even the five elements can harm him. Not even *Brahmastra* can have any effect on him, except for a few moments only as a mark of respect towards the *astra*. Everybody was satisfied with the happy turn of events. Anjaneya is thus an immortal.

destination. That is the only explanation with which I could satisfy myself. Because, this is the same feeling I also had when I first met Anjaneya in the forest. That was many years earlier and before I joined the king's army.

On one hot day in summer, I was carrying my old parents over my shoulders from *Kishkindha* to my dwelling place in the forest. To quench their thirst, I first safely put them on a big boulder and went to a pond nearby to fetch water. I felt no sense of danger till I suddenly caught sight of a huge crocodile swiftly coming towards me from the bottom of the pond. With the lazy state of my mind at that moment, it was impossible for me to escape its vicious attack. I thought it was my last moment and was concerned about my helpless parents above. Before I could think of anything to protect myself, I was surprised by the sight of the crocodile which was suddenly got hit by some object that went past me like an arrow and pierced into its open mouth. It was a huge tree trunk that split the crocodile's head fiercely and the death was instantaneous. I recovered from my shock, looked around and saw him. He is a huge *vanara* and his size is enormous. He was standing exactly behind me on the bank few feet above. His face which was facing the sun was shining like a fire ball and was registered in my mind with such a strong conviction that I could only feel that he is my God. I could not hear what he said in that hazy state of my mind. Before I could move up and reach the top, he was not seen. My father told me that he is Anjaneya and is a close associate of king Sugreeva. Somehow, from thence, a divine impression was imprinted in my mind about him. I could now feel that he developed the same towards *Rama* when he had first met the latter.

Crocodile killed by Anjaneya to rescue the *vanara* Achala

There afterwards, information had swiftly gone around the forest about the strong bond that developed between our king and the two princes and promise of the latter about liberation of Sugreeva from his grief borne out of fear from his brother Vali. This was surely a moment of joy for all. The news must have reached Vali's ears through his proteges. It was learnt in our circles that he was sufficiently warned by the queen *Tara* against any aggressive move from him. Despite that, when Sugreeva on *Rama*'s advice enticed his brother for a fight, he readily accepted and he scarcely knew that he was inviting his own death on the day. *Rama*'s arrow pierced his heart and he met the destined final moment of his death. It was a moment of sacred truth for all – victory of *Dharma over Adharma*[58].

58 *Dharma* means to be virtuous and *adharma* is opposite of dharma. As is obvious, there always exists a bitter confrontation between *dharma* and

Nevertheless, with Angada, the son of Vali standing speechless and completely crestfallen, near his father's slain body with folded hands and the queen *Tara* falling over husband's body and deeply wailing, it was a moment of utter sorrow for all of us without any exception. It obviously grieved Sugreeva also who was in a perplexed and confused state and still not able to digest the death of his brother with whom he shared a long period of happy and loving years till the evil fate separated them and left them as utter foes. At this moment, every one present might have felt the same thought: had Vali understood his brother's innocence and truthfulness and forgiven him for his folly, the events would have been quite different and never would have come to this sorrowful end for Sugreeva and Angada and his mother. Truly, God willed otherwise!

1.3 Sri Rama in grief for Sita Devi – a Divine's longing for a devotee!

I had almost had the fortune of seeing the daily routine of the two princes from very close quarters. My happiness is accentuated by the presence of Anjaneya for most of the time in the forest near to the two noble brothers. He is looking after all their needs - either on his own or by an errand from the king Sugreeva, I am unaware of. But, how much blessed I am to be near to these Divine princes!. Everyday I followed them wherever they go. In the morning, I put flowers

---

adharma. It is no surprise that these two qualities may coexist in one being itself. *Paramaatma* declares in *Bhagavad Gita* (*sloka* 8, Chapter 4):

परित्राणाय साधूनां विनाशाय च दुष्कृताम्। धर्मसंस्थापनार्थाय सम्भवामि युगे युगे॥4.8॥	Meaning of the verse – For the protection of the good (dharma), for the destruction of the wicked (beings with Adharma) and for the establishment of righteousness, I am born in every age

with lot of care near the *Pampa*[59] *sarovar* (lake) where Rama and Lakshmana perform their prayers conscientiously with Anjaneya sitting very reverently near to them. I am getting so overwhelmed by this familiar sight every day and by his (Anjaneya's) deep devotion towards the princes. I had seen him many a time in these days sitting near the entrance to the cave where the two princes are given shelter, immersing himself in deep prayer and singing in his sweet voice:

Sri Rama Sri Rama Sri Rama Sri Rama Sri Rama Sri Rama Sri Rama Sri Rama
Sri Rama Sri Rama Sri Rama Sri Rama Sri Rama Sri Rama Sri Rama Sri Rama

The sweet voice is carried by the sun rays passing through the thick cluster of trees to all surroundings with the whole forest filled with its effervescence. It is an eternal voice. Hearing to the chanting of my master, I was carried away into a trance - he is my master and he is everything for me and I am his devotee. He is an *avatar* (incarnation) of *Shiva*[60], my father used to tell me. Being such a mighty personality, how he can be so humble!. In my father's words, it is *ananya bhakti*[61] that closes the distance between the devotee and the Divine.

---

59 The location of Kishkindha coincides with Hampi that was capital of the Vijayanagar Empire. Sri Rama visited the *Pampa Sarovar* on whose bank was the *Rishyamuka* mountain. The Tungabhadra River (or Pampa) passes through these hillocks and boulders.

60 In *Shiva purana*, Anjaneya is mentioned as an avatar of *Lord.* It is said that *Shiva* in the avatar of Anjaneya helps *Lord Vishnu* (Sri Rama) to destroy the evil afflicting the earth. *Shiva* decided to be born as *Hanuman*, the son of *Vayu* the wind god and the *Apsara Anjana*, who was born on earth as a *vanara* princess due to a curse. Like *Sri Rama* who was unaware that he is none other than God's incarnation, Anjaneya had no idea he was an *avatar* (incarnation) of Lord Shiva.

61 Any being with *ananya bhakti* on the divine may not bear the separation from HIM. In *Bhagavad Gita*, the *sloka* 8 of chapter 8 describes the culmination of such a worshipper. The *sloka* reads:

Pampa *sarovar* (lake)

Chanting of Sri Rama by Anjaneya reverberating through the trees

One day the whole forest shivered and reverberated with a fierce sound which some of us could easily understand to be the thunderous sound that has come out of a mighty *dhanush* (bow) plucked by a fierce archer.

He is none other than Lakshmana, whom we found in a ferocious disposition swiftly walking towards *Kishkindha* with his bow, which, we saw all the while, was so humbly carried over his back and which at this present moment looked so massive and unconquerable and is stretched towards the sky as if it is aimed to pierce it and split it into pieces. Later, it was learnt that he was so frustrated by the sluggishness and laziness being shown by our king Sugreeva in keeping up his promise made to *Rama* that he would marshal, soon after Vali's death and his reinstatement as the king of *Kishkindha*, all his forces and send them in search of *Sita* and her abductor. This is

---

अभ्यासयोगयुक्तेन चेतसा नान्यगामिना। परमं पुरुषं दिव्यं याति पार्थानुचिन्तयन्॥8.8॥	<u>Meaning of the verse:</u> Engaged in the Yoga of constant practice of *dhyana* on *Paramaatma* and not allowing the mind to wander away to anything else, he who meditates on the supreme, and the sublime *Purusha* reaches HIM

In *Shivanandalahari* - a unique composition by *Adi Shankaracharya, sloka* 77 reads:

बुद्धिः- स्थिरा भवितुम्-ईश्वर-पाद-पद्म सक्ता वधूर्-विरहिणीव सदा स्मरन्ती सद्-भावना-स्मरण-दर्शन-कीर्तनादि सम्मोहितेव शिव-मन्त्र-जपेन विन्ते ||77||	Meaning of the verse: O Iswara! To get secured to your lotus feet, my mind always chants your name as if in a trance and it gets worried. This resembles a sweetheart separated from her lover, always remembers, contemplates, recollects of early meetings and sings about it

definitely a gross error in judgement on the part of the king and is no doubt unpardonable.

1.4 Anjaneya's search for Sita - A devotee's search for another devotee in distress

Events that swiftly followed showed the speed with which the king tried to correct his slipup. All the army was duly assembled and instructions passed to summon *vanaras* of all species from the nook and corner of the globe and muster all their strength to fulfil the task on hand. In a short time, to our bewilderment, all the forests around *Kishkindha* were soon filled up with trillions of *vanaras* who made their appearance solely because of their respect as well as the fear they had towards Sugreeva.

My fortune was on my side and I was included in the *vanara yodhas* (monkey warriors) led by Angada, our young prince of *Kishkindha* and directed by the mighty *Jambavantha* and my master Anjaneya. The other prominent personalities are Neela, Vrishabh, Maind and Dwid. We are ordained to go towards south. Soon, we proceeded on our holy task and have indeed made quick progress in exploring and searching many areas that included islands small and big, invulnerable thick forests, dangerous mountainous, terrains and deep gorges. Many *yojanas* we might have covered during this search. In the whole journey we are continuously kept in high alert by the senior *yodhas* in the party to face any hardship, an obstacle or danger. During the whole of the journey, I am so overjoyed to be able to closely observe Anjaneya's activities. I am praying to my Gods to keep me under his shadow forever. But things must have to reach an end.

Facing a futile search thus far and also with the time limit given to us already being crossed, Angada was very disappointed and was even contemplating to end his life. At that time, as if God-sent, our luck returned in the form of *Sampathi*, the brother of *Jatayu*, the mighty bird who tried to fight with *Ravana* when the latter was kidnapping *Sita* and who sacrificed his life in the valiant scuffle with the fleeing abductor. *Sampathi*, grieving for his brother's death, revealed to our relief and delight the news that he had also seen *Ravana* carrying *Sita* swiftly towards *Lanka* over the other side of the ocean.

Revitalized, we proceeded further towards south. But we soon found ourselves face-to-face with an ocean which is so vast that we could only see the sky arching down and merging with its endless expanse and with nothing beyond. While it seemed for most of us to be the end of our journey, this time it is Angada who tried to infuse into us the much needed fillip and interest in finding a solution to the task confronting us. Indeed, in the end, it is my master Anjaneya who lifted himself from his seemingly-low-profile attitude and vowed to cross the ocean, explore *Lanka,* the vicious Ravana's abode and successfully return with the good tidings about *Sita*. Of course, Jambavantha is the main motivating power behind the resurfacing of the innate energy possessed by Anjaneya. Jambavantha reminded him of his divine birth due to *Vayudeva*[62], of the indomitable courage and strength inherent in him and the necessary fortitude lying within him in successfully completing any task he is engaged in. None of us was surprised by hearing my master's extra-ordinary abilities and super-natural powers but his humility and simplicity always mystified everyone. When he really is gearing up to fly over the ocean, I am almost in a dazed state. My insides are burning up with emotion and I am concerned about the impending separation from him. He, being a *kamarupi*[63], assumed a gigantic form of many folds

62 God incarnation of wind (see also foot notes 57 and 60)

63 power in a being to be able to take any appearance he wishes

of his size and leaped onto the nearby *Mahendra giri*[64]. Announcing in his loud voice that he, even if *Sita* is not found, would definitely bring *Ravana* as a captive and return from *Lanka with a success.* We all saw him, with awe and rapt attention, taking off from the mountain's tip at top speed. That was the last sight of him I had till I had a glimpse of him coming back towards us with a mountainous roar at the end of almost two nights and a day.

Anjaneya crossing the ocean on the way to Lanka

During this period of his absence, I visited *Mahendra giri* countless number of times unseen by my colleagues and roamed around like

64 *Mahendra giri* is a mountain on the southern end of India from which Anjaneya took a leap to reach *Lanka* on the other side of the ocean. It is Sugreeva *(slokas* 4-41-1 to 4-41-49, *Kishkindha kanda, Ramayana* of *Valmiki)* who gave a graphic description to his *vanara yodhas (for whom* Angada *was made the chief)* of the possible route they need to take to south of Vindhya mountains and reach the island *Lanka* - a dazzling island on the other side of the shore of Mountain *Mahendra,* which they need to search for Sita devi up to its fringes.

a dazed animal. I was going on spelling his name within myself and offering prayers for his safe return. I could hear my heart rhythmically throbbing with a continuous prayer on him:

[65]मनोजवं मारुततुल्यवेगं
जितेन्द्रियं बुद्धिमतां वरिष्ठ।
वातात्मजं वानरयूथमुख्यं
श्रीरामदूतं शरणं प्रपद्ये

Soon, when I caught sight of his return from a distance, I ran down the mountain at light speed howling at the top of my voice, dancing with joy, falling in between and crawling on all fours. Before I could reach my people, to my surprise and shock, I found his gigantic feet almost above my head in the sky and himself reaching them before I could.

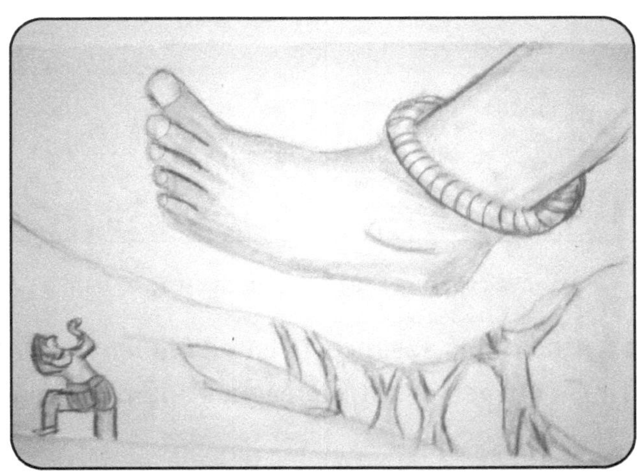

Anjaneya returning from Lanka after visiting Sita devi

65 Meaning of the verse: I salute my ideal deity Anjaneya who is swift as the mind and fast as the wind, who is the master of the senses, who is known for his exceptional intelligence, learning and wisdom and who is the son of the wind God and chief among the *vanaras*. From that messenger of *Sri Rama*, the God incarnate, I seek for refuge by prostrating before him.

1.5 Anjaneya's momentous return from Lanka with grand message to the Divine Sri Rama

Joy erupted in the mountains when Anjaneya revealed that Rama's *dhrama patni*[66] Sita *devi* is safe but is under seize and is being protected by *asuras* in *Ravana*'s *Lanka*. When he started describing all the events that followed his departure from us, we all listened to him with all attention and got bewildered by his superlative and admirable actions performed with supreme wisdom. In all this narrative, my common-place intellect also was particularly awe-struck by a couple of situations described by him. One is his magnificent quality of treating all other *vanara yodhas* with high esteem and belittling himself instead. This is reflected in his own words by which he described to Sita devi[67] the indomitable supremacy possessed by his colleague *vanaras* in *Kishkindha* (Sarga 39, Sundara kanda):

मत् विशिष्टाः च तुल्याः च सन्ति तत्र वन ओकसः।
मत्तः प्रत्यवरः कश्चिन् न अस्ति सुग्रीव सम्निधौ॥

Meaning that *"In them, some of the monkeys are superior to me and some are even equal to me. No one in the vicinity of* Sugreeva *is inferior to me".*

An unparalleled self-faith and devotion towards Sri Rama it is!. His in-born qualities of strength and shrewdness are his weapons. Another captivating aspect we learnt from him is Sita devi's conviction about herself. In her own words (as described by Anjaneya), it is reflected thus:

66 A virtuous, dutiful and righteous wife

67 The word '*devi*' is added to the lady *Sita* signifying her splendid character and her infallible faith in her husband – the divine *Sri Rama*

शक्या लोभयितुं नाहमैश्वर्येण धनेन वा
अनन्या राघवेणाहं भास्करेण प्रभा यथा
अहमौपयीकी भार्या तस्यैव वसुधापतेः
व्रतस्नातस्य विप्रस्य विद्येव विदितात्मनः
(Sarga 21, Sundara kanda)

These are the words, it seems, she spoke while addressing the cruel *Ravana;* meaning that *she is inseparable from Sri Rama*[68] *in the same way as sun-shine is from the sun and that she is fit only to Sri Rama like the vidya (knowledge) of an accomplished ascetic. And, she is not capable to be tempted by wealth or by money and she is a suitable wife to that Sri Rama alone, the lord of earth.* A remarkable lady indeed!.

I am not all surprised by my master's valiant encounters with the *asuras* and *Ravana* and the grandeur he displayed in performing his duty as a *Sri Rama duta*[69]. Even when he conveyed the precious message to Sri Rama about Sita devi's safe disposition in *Lanka* even though she is under constant watch and harassment by *asuras*, my master displayed remarkable restraint. This is also according to the well-professed advice (- about the need to be circumspect in the presence of the royal princes) received from Jambavantha before reaching the abode of Sri Rama and his brother Lakshmana. While placing the true facts before his Lord, Anjaneya intelligently soothed him too, by saying that Sita *devi* got pacified by his (Anjaneya's) assurances and promises that, soon after his return to *Kishkindha*

68 In what more splendid words, a relationship/union between a husband and wife can be described! In the mind of a devotee (Sita devi), it is a union with the Divine and is something very much beyond the commonplace way of thinking. It is transcendental and eternal.

69 messenger from *Sri Rama*

and his appraising Sri Rama of her plight, the prince accompanied by his brother Lakshmana and Sugreeva would soon arrive in *Lanka* with the *akhanda vanara sena*[70] and secure her freedom after killing *Ravana* and all his kith and kin.

Anjaneya giving anguliyakam (ring) to Sita devi

70 On Sugreeva's order, all *vanaras* and *bhallukaas* (bears) residing in different parts of the earth arrived in *Kishkindha* in the shortest time possible. Sugreeva describes to *Sri Rama* the valiant character of the millions of *vanaras* who assembled before them in the following verses (in Ramayana written by *sage Valmiki*) :

ख्यात कर्म अपदानाः च बलवन्तो जित क्लमाः पराक्रमेषु विख्याता व्यवसायेषु च उत्तमाः॥ पृथिवि अंबु चरा राम नाना नग निवासिनः। कोटि ओघाः च इमे प्राप्ता वानराः तव किंकराः । 4-40-4, 5	Meaning of the verses: Oh, Rama, these *vanaras* are acclaimed for undertaking impossible deeds, and they will accomplish whatever task they have undertaken. They are powerful ones who have overcome weariness. They are renowned for their confrontation and noteworthy in their manoeuvres. These *vanaras* who are the dwellers on diverse mountains can travel either on earth or on water. They have come in millionfold as your servants

1.6 *Epic fight between the Divine and the Devil – Anjaneya's unique devotion to Sri Rama*

For all the *vanara yodhas*, it is a joyous moment and also a blessed one to prove their faith and mettle to their king Sugreeva in the ensuing war with *asuras*. It was a boisterous and adventurous journey we all made to reach *Lanka* with the help of a *setu* (bridge) built across the mighty ocean. This was made possible because of the advice received from *Samudra*, the king of oceans, that the *setu* can be cleverly constructed by mere boulders utilizing the construction skills of *Nala*[71], son of *Viswakarma* (architect in heaven).

Once we crossed the ocean, war soon started. The war is between good and evil, d*harma* and *adharma* and the virtuous and the sinner. It was remarkable that Sri Rama, following *kshatriya dharma*[72], sent Angada as a messenger to the court of Ravana before the start of the war to warn him, but, of course, as expected by us all, it fell on deaf ears of Ravana (who is oblivious to the impending fierce consequences awaiting him from the war). Throughout the epic fight, two or three *things* stand out as mirroring the divine qualities of Sri Rama and the unstinted devotion of Sita *devi* and Anjaneya.

---

71 *Nala* is a *vanara* in Sugreeva's army and is a son of *Vishawakarma* (a divine architect in heaven). It is an engineering marvel that *Nala* constructed the bridge over the ocean of 100 *yojanas* (800 miles) with boulders and logs of wood in 5 days (according to Valmiki Ramayana) so that Rama and his army could cross the ocean and easily reach *Lanka*.

72 While a *kshatriya* is bound to protect the society under him and establish *dharma* by punishing the wrong doers, it is also a noble quality to give the opponent an opportunity to come fully prepared for a fight and it is a nothing but a sublime quality not to attack the enemy when he is exhausted and tired on the battle field.

First, my master's faith and devotion towards his Lord got rewarded when Sri Rama sat over his shoulders almost throughout the battle and fought with *asuras* and Ravana. How much blessed my master was and it was, no doubt, a *union between a devotee and the divine and a confluence of an aatma*[73] *with Paramaatma.*

It was again a glorious moment in my master's life when he was required to go to Himalayas and bring the magical medicinal

73 union between and a confluence of a self and supreme self:

In the following *sloka*s 15 and 20, Chapter 6 of *Bhagavad Gita*, Bhagawaan Sri Krishna explains

युञ्जन्नेवं सदात्मानं योगी नियतमानसः। शान्तिं निर्वाणपरमां मत्संस्थामधिगच्छति॥ 6.15 यत्रोपरमते चित्तं निरुद्धं योगसेवया। यत्र चैवात्मनात्मानं पश्यन्नात्मनि तुष्यति॥ 6.20	Meaning of the verses: By a continued practice of *dhyana yoga* (practice of meditation) attains withdrawal of mind and intellect from the worldly objects, reaches a state of quietude, realizes union with the Supreme *aatma* and enjoys the eternal and *atindriya* (supersensuous) bliss. (*Aatma* or *jivaatma* is the *chaitanyam* (vitality)/life in a body)

Also, in *sloka* 22, Chapter 8:

पुरुषः स परः पार्थ भक्त्या लभ्यस्त्वनन्यया। यस्यान्तःस्थानि भूतानि येन सर्वमिदं ततम्॥ 8.22	Meaning of the verse: HE, in whom all beings abide and by whom the entire universe is pervaded, can be attained only by *ananya bhakti* (undistracted devotion) directed to HIM alone.

If we also refer to Dakshinamurty *stotram* (prayer) of Adi Sankaracharya, we find a unique description of the supreme confluence in this following *sloka*:

plants[74] to save Lakshmana when he fell unconscious during his fight with *Indrajit*, the son of *Ravana*. It was a fortune for some of

---

<table>
<tr><td>मौनव्याख्या प्रकटित परब्रह्मतत्त्वं युवानं वर्षिष्ठांतेव सद्ऋषिगणैः आवृतं ब्रह्मनिष्ठैः
आचार्येन्द्रं करकलित चिन्मुद्रमानंदमूर् स्वात्मारामं मुदितवदनं दक्षिणामूर्तिमीडे</td><td></td></tr>
<tr><td colspan="2"><u>Meaning of the verse:</u> Dakshinamurty is the teacher of teachers. This great teacher held his hand in the sign of knowledge, i.e., CIN mudra shown in the figure stands for the non-verbal communication through silence by Dakshina Murty advising his disciples to give up the natural tendency of identifying oneself with the body, mind and indriyaas (sensory organs) but try to merge with Paramaatma thus perceiving the divinity within and attaining aatmasanyamam, i.e, self-realization and thus the eternal bliss.</td></tr>
</table>

74 When Anjaneya arrived in the Himalayas to gather this life-saving herb but could not identify sanjeevani (the plant that is supposed to be a life-saving herb), he uprooted a part of the mountain and carried it to Lanka. The Vedic hymn in Tenth Mandala (10-97) of Rig Veda mentions 107 herbs. Mandala means 'book'. Even though the names of these 107 herbs are not known, one can come across hundreds of herbs in the Ayurvedic books of Charaka and Susrutha. Charaka and Susrutha are renowned physicians in ancient India. Atharvana Veda contains talismans for herbs for healthy life. Charaka Samhita, which is a handbook of Aurveda, contains a comprehensive literature on the practice and its core philosophy includes anatomy of human body, diagnosis and prognosis and specialized treatment methods.

According to the legend, many medicinal miracles are associated with Himalayan herbs. There exist many such herbs that have high medicinal values. However, no authentic documentation is available about their medicinal properties – even though each plant growing at such altitudes may be a miraculous sanjeevani. Himalayas of India are treated as a precious treasury of medicinal herbs and plants (Joshi et al. 2016. Himalayan Aromatic Medicinal Plants: A Review of their Ethnopharmacology, Volatile Phytochemistry, and Biological Activities, Medicines (Basel), Vol. 3(1). 6) and (Medicinal and Aromatic Plant Science and Biotechnology, 2010. Ed. A M Husaini. Global Science Books, Ltd.).

us when we were also severely injured and were almost breathing our last. We all got immediately rejuvenated by mere inhaling of the fragrance of the medicines and it was a new life given to us by the mercy of Sri Rama, the divine incarnate and his dedicated devotee Anjaneya.

Anjaneya bringing Rsabhadri mountain with medicinal plants

We were all surprised and overwhelmed by the majestic display of divinity by Sri Rama, when he asked his unholy and vicious rival *Ravana* to go back from the battle field (when the latter was seen to be fatigued and tired), to take rest and to come back to fight with him. After losing all his prominent *asuras* and brother *Kumbhakarna* and all his sons also in the war, it ought to have been a moment of truth and a reality for *Ravana* to realize at least at that instant the imminent consequence of the war and the dire prospects of losing his life. Instead, in consequence to his predominant *rajo guna*[75], he displayed his folly and finally embraced his death in the hands of divine Sri Rama.

1.7 Sita's display of her achanchala bhakti (unwavering devotion) towards the divine Sri Rama

It was a very sorrowful and shocking moment for all the *vanaras* when Sri Rama tells Sita devi that after she lived in Ravana's *Lanka* for such a long period away from him, he is averse to take her back and she can go anywhere she likes. It was an equally a furious moment for some including Lakshmana who threw a vivid look of unhappiness at his beloved brother Sri Rama. It so happened that some of us were seriously injured in the war, isolated and taken care of under constant medicinal attention in a nearby place. However, all that that happened soon after the war, I was fortunate enough to learn much later from some of those blessed senior *vanaras*.

1.7.1 The devotee's (*Sita devi's*) mind towards the Divine

On that memorable day, all the puzzled and immensely worried onlookers might have construed that Sita devi, with innumerable thoughts crowding her mind must have gone into her own world of despair. But, the peaceful and exceptionally radiant and calm countenance on her face decipherable only to few blessed souls

75 *rajo guna* is one of the three *gunas* (attributes) acquired by a being by birth; As clearly elucidated by *Paramaatma* in the verse 37, Chapter 3, Bhagavad Gita, *kamam* (desire) arises from *rajo guna* that ultimately leads one to complete downfall. Tthe *sloka* reads as:

काम एष क्रोध एष रजोगुणसमुद्भवः। महाशनो महापाप्मा विद्ध्येनमिह वैरिणम्॥ 3.37	Meaning of the verse: *Kama* i.e., desire is all sinful and destroying; one should know this as the fearful enemy in this mortal life

around indicates that she is actually in a state of profound elation with the sole thought of having got at last an opportunity to be dear and near to her Divine. Along with this thought she has also gone into her own reverie dwelling into her past. She, as a loving daughter of King *Janaka* was in perpetual prayers with a fervent wish to woo only the Divine. With her wish fulfilled after winning Sri Rama as her husband, she has entered into the kingdom of *Raghu vamsa*[76] as the eldest daughter-in-law of *King Dasaradha* and had an unforgettable stint of wedded and contented life till she accompanied her husband to *Dandakarnya* to lead a life of exile for fourteen years. As a devotee adorns, worships and follows the Divine God wholly by *manasa, vaacha* and *karmana*[77], she has lived in the forest with all peace and contentment and served Sri Rama with all her attention rivetted on him. All the moments of her intimacy with the Divine Sri Rama got etched in her memory. The flowers, the birds and even the rivulets she bathed in, remained as her sweet companions. All the precincts of her small dwelling place in the forest, according to her, surely must have defined the God's sublime abode. She even cherished with utmost relish the episode of *kakasura*[78] and the seemingly unhappy

---

76 It is considered to be an offshoot of the lineage of kings, tracing its ancestry to the sun deity. *Raghu vaṃsa* kings include Mandhata, Harishchandra, Sagara, Bhagiratha, Dilipa, Raghu, Aja, Dasaratha, Sri Rama

77 By thought, speech and action

78 When Hanuman asked Sita *devi* to give him a token of remembrance so that he can convince Sri Rama that he indeed met her, then she narrated this story of *kakasura* to him. It happened when She and Sri Rama were staying near Chitrakuta forest. On one day, when they are taking rest, a crow, yearning for meat, began to peck her chest. When she screamed, Sri Rama woke up and saw the blood-stained nails of the crow, he was angry and took a *kusa* grass or *darbha* grass, murmured the Brahmastra mantra and threw the grass on the crow. It started chasing the crow. The crow ran everywhere for faer of its life and finally came to Sri Rama only and

encounter with a *vayasam* (crow) when she had tasted the nectar of the protective charm of her Divine. The visit of the *tapasvini* Anasuya[79], the wife of sage Atri and her soothing influence on Sita devi's life in the forest assumes significance in this regard. Also, with unflinching faith in her beloved Divine husband, she could spend her appalling imprisonment in *Ravan*a's kingdom in *Lanka* with utmost forbearance. Her chiding the wicked *Ravana* in both soft and the most harshest fashion[80] stands as an epitome of her infallible chastity and undaunted courage. Her expression of anguish and loss of self-confidence at times in those crucifying moments of disappointment are only indications of momentary

surrendered. The Brahmastra cannot be taken back. But, since Si Rama pardoned the crow, he saved it by allowing Brahmastra to hit only one eye of the crow.

79 Anasuya was the wife of sage Atri and like her name, she was free of feelings like jealousy, anger, envy and leading a peaceful life (canto 3 of Maha Bhagavatam of Veda Vyasa) with her husband in a small hermitage located in the southern part of the Chitrakuta forest. According to the legend, the Trimurti – Brahma, Vishnu and Shiva turned themselves into Anusuya's son – Sri Dattatreya.

80 The following *slokas* in Sundarkanda of Srimad Ramayana by sage Valmiki display her fortitude and courage in facing the wicked Ravana:

असंदेशात्तु रामस्य तपसश्चामपालनात्। न त्वां कुर्मि दशग्रीव भस्म भस्माहर्तेजसा॥ २२ - २०	Oh Ravana! I have not reduced you to ashes for your unforgivable utterances through the power of my chastity, since I do not have my Lord's permission
क्षिप्रं तव स नाथो मे रामः सौमित्रिणा सह॥ ५-२१-३३ तोयमल्पमिवादित्यः प्रानानादास्यते शरैः।	My husband Sri Rama together with Lakshmana will take away with His arrows your life quickly as the sun dries up shallow water

disillusionment[81] on the part of a devotee caused by the pangs of separation from the Supreme and Divine savior.

Now, when Sita devi, a true-devotee-incarnate has the injunction from her Divine that she can go anywhere she likes and he is averse to take her back, an occasion has come for the devotee to express total surrender to HIM which is the ultimate state of *ananya bhakti* (unflinching devotion). Soon, the grand lady immediately opted to jump into fire and prove her infallible devotion towards HIM, the Supreme.

How much worthy and holy the actions must have been in their earlier births, of all the *vanaras* and other onlookers present on that holy land in those crucial and astounding moments! The next few moments of their lives brought them close to a divine sight when all sovereign God incarnations – *Maha Shiva*[82], *Brahma*[83], *Mahendra*[84], *Kubera*[85], *Yama*[86], *Varuna*[87] made their appearance before Sri Rama and exhorted him to recognize his incarnation of *Lord Narayana* (*Paramaatma and the Supreme Almighty*) and the glorious purpose for which he has taken birth in this universe. They proclaim his divinity and eulogize him with the hymns:

81

न हि मे जीविते नार्थो नै वार्थैर्न च भूषणैः। वसन्त्या राक्षसीमध्ये विना रामं महारथम्॥ ५-२६-५	By living in the midst of these *asuras* (demons) without Sri Rama, there is no use with life to me; nor with wealth nor with ornaments

82 *Maha Shiva* - God's incarnation as a destroyer of whole universe

83 *Brahma* - God's incarnation as a procreator of the whole universe

84 *Mahendra* - God's incarnation in control of heaven

85 *Kubera* - God's incarnation in control of riches/wealth

86 *Yama* - God's incarnation in control of hell and so on extinction/death of all beings

87 *Varuna* - God's incarnation in control of rains

कर्ता सर्वस्य लोकस्य श्रेष्ठो ज्ञानवतां प्रभुः।
उपेक्षसे कथं सीतां पतन्तीं हव्यवाहने॥
कथं देवगणश्रेष्ठमात्मानं नावबुद्ध्यसे | Sarga 117-6

(Meaning of the verse: "How do you, the maker of the entire cosmos, the foremost among those endowed with knowledge and an all-capable person, ignore Sita who is falling into the fire? How do you not recognize yourself to be the foremost of the troop of gods?")

अन्ते चादौ च लोकानां दृश्यसे च परंतप॥
उपेक्षसे च वैदेहीं मानुषः प्राकृतो यथा। Sarga 117-9

(Meaning of the verse: "O the destroyer of the adversaries. You are seen (to exist) at the beginning and at the end of creation. Yet, you ignore Sita, just like a common man.")

सीता लक्ष्मीर्भवान् विष्णुर्देवः कृष्णः प्रजापतिः॥
वधार्थं रावणस्येह प्रविष्टो मानुषीं तनुम्। Sarga 117-28

(Meaning of the verse: "*Sita* is no other than *Goddess Lakshmi* (the divine consort of *Lord Vishnu*), while you are *Lord Vishnu*. You are having a shining dark-blue hue. You are the *Lord* of created beings. For the destruction of *Ravana*, you entered a human body here, on this earth.")

The very God *Agni* who presides over all sacred fire in this world also appeared before Sri Rama and presented the *maha sadhvi*[88] Sita

88 *maha sadhvi* means an accomplished lady. Here, one must recognize all superlative qualities in a woman - *distinction, success, speech, memory, intelligence, firmness and forgiveness* as *Paramaatma's* glories only (*sloka* 34, chapter 10, Bhagavad Gita). Specifically on a higher plane of thinking, one

devi in an unscathed and in her pristine form to Lord Rama with the words:

नैव वाचा न मनसा नैव बुद्ध्या न चक्षुषा। सुवृत्ता वृत्तशौण्डीर्यं न त्वामत्यचरच्छुभा॥ (Yuddha kanda118.6)	Meaning of the verse: This auspicious lady, whose character has been good, has never been unfaithful to you and endowed with strength of character either by word or by mind or even by intellect or by her glances."
विशुद्धभावां निष्पापां प्रतिगृह्णीष्व मैथिलीम्। न किंचिरभिधातव्या अहमाज्ञापयामि ते॥ (Yuddha kanda118.10)	Meaning of the verse: Take back Sita who is sinless, with a pure character. She should not be told anything harsh. I hereby command you."

Final moments of reunion of the devotee Sita devi and the divine Sri Rama

Sri Rama gloriously heeded to the salutary advice from the affectionate guardians of the world. Finally, it is a magnificent moment for all *vanaras* and all the witnessing Godly incarnations to behold the grand event of Sri Rama, the highly illustrious scion of *Raghu* dynasty getting reunited with her beloved Sita *devi*.

---

needs to recognize that all manifestations emanate from the one and only one Omnipresent, Omniscient, All-pervading Almighty as evident from the following *sloka* 39, chapter 10, Bhagavad Gita:

यच्चापि सर्वभूतानां बीजं तदहमर्जुन । न तदस्ति विना यत्स्यान्मया भूतं चराचरम् ॥ 10.39 ॥	Meaning of the verse: Whatsoever is the seed of all beings, that also am I; there is no being, whether moving or unmoving that can exist without Me

1.8 Anjaneya's paramanandabhuti (sublime bliss) and his eternal meditation:

(Sri Rama Sri Rama Sri Rama Sri Rama Sri Rama)

When my master Anjaneya returned from *Ayodhya* after the celebrating moment of the princely coronation ceremony was over with Sri Rama crowned as the king of this *Prithvi* (earth), I have found him in a new glorious mood. The mood is reminiscent of a mind dwelling in a state of fulfilment and utmost satisfaction. In recent times, his visits to *Kishkindha* and meetings with the king Sugreeva became few and far between. He is perpetually absorbed in a state of meditation and prayer towards the *Purushothama* [89] Sri Rama. He must be in a state of *samyamam*[90] that symbolizes the union of the two - *devotee and the Divine* - into one.

[91]*A trivial addendum to this First Part*

In the days that followed, I, *Achala*, am fortunate enough to closely follow my divine Anjaneya, to take care of his needs unobserved by him and to happily spend in the jungles, valleys and over the mountains moving with him wherever he wanders. I do not know whether my movements are noticed by him but as for myself I always have the firm view that I am unnoticed (of course, this may be untrue and a wishful thinking on my part). I am satisfied with my this short life of being and remaining as a devoted deputy to my master. My good old parents are no more and my master himself is

---

89 the most acclaimed one

90 This is a state of CIN mudra (see footnote 73)

91 Here, the *vanara Achala* is a fictitious character and is pronounced to be dumb in the last para of this first part. Let us also envision that he was fortunate enough to get enrolled in Sugreeva's *vanara* army even with this deformity because of his father's earlier supposed-to-be impeccable and loyal record in the service of the king in *Kishkindha*.

my mother, father and everything[92]. Of course, my master, unmindful of his surroundings around, is in eternal prayers on Divine Sri Rama. I consider my life also as one of fulfilment, may be on a minor/ insignificant scale. Having been afflicted by the deformity of being dumb by birth, I may be unable to offer prayers fully to my divine Anjaneya by body and speech. However, this is not at all a limitation for me in being devoted to my Divine Anjaneya at least through *manasica puja* (worship by thoughts).

Anjaneya in eternal prayers

---

92 For a devotee, the divine is everything. He tries to feel HIM as close as possible to him like a mother and father, always breath HIM and live with HIM. *Paramaatma* HIMSELF says in *Bhagavad Gita* (*sloka* 17 of Chapter 9):

पिताहमस्य जगतो माता धाता पितामहः। वेद्यं पवित्रमोङ्कार ऋक्साम यजुरेव च ॥9.17॥	Meaning of the verse: I am the father of this universe – the mother, the sustainer, the grandfather, the purifier, the knowable, the sacred mono-syllable OM and also the Rig, Sama and the Yajur Vedas)

SECOND PART

Sri Krishna, Yasoda and the Gopikas

Hare Krishna Hare Krishna
Krishna Krishna Hare Hare

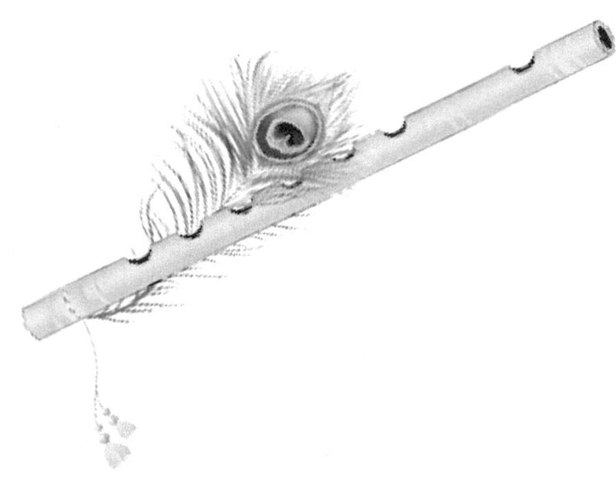

2.1 *Gokula and Yasoda, the Devotee and little Divine Krishna*

Of late, all in Gokula have a feeling that our *gokula* is experiencing a stony silence. Obvious is the reason - all are worried about the series of recent disasters that befell on our otherwise peaceful dwelling place. More worried all of us on noticing that these are directly connected with our little loving Krishna. Many *asura* type of people came to our place in recent times *in different devilish forms*[93] with the only intention of harming Krishna. To the surprise of all, all these cruel people met their ghastly death instantly and how this has happened, nobody has any clear idea. But we are all wonderstruck and at the same time relieved with immense joy to find our beloved Krishna unhurt and remaining playful. Our Yasoda *tayi* and *Nanda maharaj*[94], how much they are suffering and feeling unhappy with these incidents, it is beyond anybody's guess. It is no more a secret for all in Gokula that Kamsa, the king of *Madhura*[95] is behind these gory incidents because of his premonition and *fear of death*[96] from our beloved Krishna.

"*Achala*, go and fetch a bowl of ghee from Yasoda *tayi*", my mother called from inside. I came out of my little reverie and ran out. My house is at the end of our street and is small in size compared to others. It is my place and I like it. It has flower plants on either side

93 See footnote 44. On command from king Kamsa, different asuras – Putaki as a young lady, Trinavarta in the form of whirlwind, Aghasura in the form of a python came to Gokula to kill Krishna. Each one of them faced their death in the hands of Krishna.

94 Yasoda and Nanda are Krishna's foster parents. Here '*tayi*' means mother and '*maharaj*' means chieftain. Nanda is the chief of all the dwellers in *Gokulum*. *Vasudeva* and *Devaki* are the real parents to Krishna.

95 See footnote 39

96 See footnote 44

in the front place, some trees and a well in back of the house and a place reserved for our few cows and their calves in the foreground.

In recent times whenever I go and visit Yasoda *tayi,* I find anxiety writ large on her face. It is understandable and I always wish to dissuade her from grief borne out of her imaginations, even though I am very young compared to her age. Also, what knowledge I possess to exchange my viewpoints, suppose, on philosophy of this life with a grown-up lady of such exemplary faith and devotion. She is a remarkable and extremely blessed lady *as I learnt*[97] from my parents. I generally know from my close association and movements with other ladies in *Gokula* and with *gopikas*[98] of my age that for Yasoda *tayi,* the little Krishna is everything and he is her life's savior and divine.

Krishna in his childhood chivalry

97 See footnotes 94 and 99

98 Village belles in Gokula

Krishna also, has his own inimitable adolescent way of making his mother believe him absolutely. Her belief in him is unshakeable and complete like a devotee having *ananya bhakti* (unwavering devotion) towards his divine benefactor.

Yasoda *tayi*'s house is on the main street and as I approached it, I became alert since I know the little Krishna is quite mischievous. Some small monkeys are roaming around the ground and they looked at me with a blank face but I can see their gleeful eyes with a look of playfulness natural to them. When I slowly went inside the house, I found Krishna cuddling in his mother's lap and I could see her *happily cajoling him with all affection*[99]. Suddenly, I observed Krishna opening his mouth and was surprised by the expression on Yasoda *tayi*'s face displaying a mix of bewilderment and disbelief. At that moment, I was at a loss to understand the reason but the sight before me made a great imprint and got locked in my mind – Yasoda *tayi* with a bewildered face looking at Krishna in her lap with *his*

99 It is said that Yasoda and Nanda who were the virtuous couple *Drona* and *Dhara* in their earlier birth were blessed to have a birth in *manava loka* (human world) again as a wedded couple in *Gokula*. According to their wishes, they are born in *Dwapur yuga* as human beings with *achanchala bhakti* (unwavering devotion) and adoration towards *Paramaatma*, the God almighty. In this life, they were the most blessed devotees bestowed with the highest reward of rearing and cuddling the very God who is omnipresent, omniscient and otherwise not easily accessible for all. But HE is easily attainable through *bhakti*. The same is echoed in *sloka* 22, Chapter 8, *Bhagavad Gita*:

पुरुषः स परः पार्थ भक्त्या लभ्यस्त्वनन्यया । यस्यान्तःस्थानि भूतानि येन सर्वमिदं ततम् ॥ 8.22 ॥	Meaning: That Supreme Purusha, in whom all beings abide and by whom the entire universe is pervaded, can be attained by undistracted devotion directed to Him alone

small mouth open and her penetrating look of askance for a fleet of a second.

This wonderful picture in my mind reappeared before me, when Rohini *tayi*[100], mother of Balarama and sister of Yasoda *tayi* described the strange incident to the ladies some time later. It seems that, on that memorable day when I was present, Yasoda *devi* got spellbound and had seen with disbelief the whole universe in the mouth of Krishna. Strangely, the scene erased out of her mind in an instant and she also dispelled it with her usual motherly instinct of showing concern for little Krishna's health and immediately made prayers to all Gods for the well-being of Krishna.

Soon it was followed by the incident of two gigantic trees suddenly crashing down[101] in Nanda Maharaj's compound. It had greatly shaken Yasoda *tayi's* motherly instinct about the safety of little Krishna.

With some more spellbinding and enthralling events taking place in *Gokula,* we all moved over to *Brindavan*. Some blessed souls in

100 Rohini is the second wife of Nanda maharaj. After the cruel Kamsa, king of Madhura, killed six of the children begot by his sister Devaki, the *yoga maya*, under instructions of *Paramaatma* transferred Devaki's embryo (seventh one) to Rohiṇi. The child because of his great physical strength was named Balarama (chapter 2, canto10, Maha Bhagavatam of Veda Vyasa).

101 The two gigantic (Arjuna) trees are in fact, Nalakuvara and Manigriva who were the sons of demigod Kubera and who took the form of trees due to a curse from Narada Muni (chapter 10, canto 10, Maha Bhagavatam of Veda Vyasa). However, Narada Muni gave them the relief that they will regain their original forms when Lord Krishna delivers them of this curse. When little Krishna was tied to a big mortar by mother Yasoda, HE uprooted the trees by going in between them. Soon, Nalakuvara and Manigriva came out of the trees in their original form and returned to their places after offering their respectful obeisances to Lord Krishna.

Gokula could have perceived doubtlessly the superlative powers of Krishna as a young lad and his divinity. But, the decision to move out of Gokula is final and it is all owing to the reservations and fears expressed by many elders based on the vicious and deliberate attacks on the life of our Krishna. With the approval of Nanda maharaj, we finally are on our way to the new dwelling place.

2.2 Journey to Brindavan

The journey to Brindavan is so pleasant that all - young and old - put their memories of the unpleasant incidents that happened in Gokula, off their minds. I could also see a great sense of relief particularly on the joyous faces of Yasoda *tayi* and Rohini *tayi* with Balarama and Krishna immensely enjoying the ride with all the *gopalas* and *gopikas*. Yasoda *tayi* always impressed my young mind so much that for me, she is an embodiment of ideal and holy mother and in this regard she is an idol and divine to me. How much sweet voice she has and I could hear and relish her songs from close quarters on many occasions. I used to get always fascinated by her cradlesongs on Krishna:

[102]*cradle-song on Krishna:*

jo jo muvvala Krishna

jō jō navanita Krishna

jo jo muvvala Krishna *jō jō navanita Krishna*

jo jo muvvala Krishna

jo jo Devaki Krishna *jo jo Vasudeva Krishna*

jo jo muvvala Krishna *jō jō navanita Krishna*

102 The song has words from both Sanskrit and Telugu language

jo jo muvvala Krishna	
jō jō Yasoda Krishna	*jō jō Nanda Krishna*
jo jo muvvala Krishna	*jō jō navanita Krishna*
jo jo muvvala Krishna	
jo jo Gokula Krishna	*jō jō yamuna Krishna*
jo jo muvvala Krishna	*jō jō navanita Krishna*
jo jo muvvala Krishna	
jo jo murali Krishna	*jo jo mohana Krishna*
jo jo muvvala Krishna	*jō jō navanita Krishna*
jo jo muvvala Krishna	
jo jo Gopala Krishna	*jo jo Govinda Krishna*
jo jo Muvvala Krishna	*jō jō Navanita Krishna*
jo jo muvvala Krishna	

All the boys and girls of my age and above are all hilarious and playful throughout this short journey to Brindavan. In the first few bullock-carts, all the ladies are accommodated followed by carts filled with all house-hold articles. Elders and the old are put up in the last few carts. Next, cows along with their calves are herded by the *gopalas* with the able-bodied persons following behind – some silently and some engaged in loud conversations. The tinkling of cow-bells[103], the bells under the carts, the rough sounds of the cart-wheels, the slow murmuring of ladies, the showy clamors from the young and the old have filled the air with a joyous feeling of elation and celebration. The whole sight of our movement along

103 Bells tied around the cow's neck

the serpentine road and amidst the *godhuli*[104] filling the air is an exciting one for long time to remember. Krishna and Balarama, both of them are at their best in playing and dancing with all *gopalas* all through the journey. Both of them are now almost nearing their fifth year of age.

While Balarama generally keeps himself calm and less conversant, Krishna is remarkably quite flamboyant and flowery in mingling with elders even. The distinction is markedly clear. Balarama is very fair in complexion and Krishna is pronounced by his distinct color of *neela mehga* (blue clouds). With his flute tucked in his waist yellow cloth and his dark blackish hair flying over his forehead and eye brows, Krishna's demeanor even at that young age is exceptional and carries a superlative elegance beyond any description. I happened to hear with awe and wonder on many occasions my parents mentioning that Krishna is an exceptional child and is being brought up in Yasoda *tayi*'s house by God's grace. All of us have the conviction that he is a mystic child and is amongst us to our fortune.

Even though I wish to join the group of friends in their playful games, I remained with my mother in the cart reciting some poems in my dumb voice at her command. Hearing some ladies in the carts in our front singing in praise of Lord Sri Rama, my mother also has joined them and soon all ladies started singing in chorus:

104 *Dhuli* means dust and *godhuli* means dust arising from the cow's trotting on the dusty road

chorus song by the ladies on Lord Sri Rama:

Sri Rama Sri Rama	*jaya jaya Rama*	
Sri Rama Sri Rama	*jaya jaya Rama*	*Sri Rama Sri Rama jaya jaya Rama*
Raghukula Rama	*Kosala Rama*	
Ayodhya Rama	*jaya jaya Rama*	
Sri Rama Sri Rama	*jaya jaya Rama*	*Sri Rama Sri Rama, jaya jaya Rama*
Dasaratha Rama	*Pavana Rama*	
Kousalya Rama	*jaya jaya Rama*	
Sri Rama Sri Rama,	*jaya jaya Rama*	*Sri Rama Sri Rama, jaya jaya Rama*
Janaki Rama	*Kodanda Rama*	
Maruti Rama	*jaya jaya Rama*	
Sri Rama Sri Rama,	*jaya jaya Rama*	*Sri Rama Sri Rama, jaya jaya Rama*
Sri Rama Sri Rama	*jaya jaya Rama*	
Sri Rama Sri Rama,	*jaya jaya Rama*	*Sri Rama Sri Rama, jaya jaya Rama*

The whole atmosphere in the journey turned into a pious one and reverberated with the songs on Sri Rama and Anjaneya. From my childhood, both my grand-parents and parents used to tell me and my friends the grand old stories of Sri Rama. Anjaneya remains for me as my Divine God.

My thoughts are broken by the laughing sounds of all the boys who are now carrying Krishna and Balarama on their shoulders and singing in their praise accompanied by their dancing steps and followed by their intermittent joyous shouts that the two brothers are their little godly masters.

Krishna and Balarama with gopalas

2.3 Brindavan and the divine acts of Krishna

At last, the journey has come to an end. The place finally arrived and has immensely attracted everybody, as it would, firstly because of its new surroundings and environment. It is indeed a place of serene beauty covered by lush green lands around ensuring fodder for all seasons for all including the large flock of cows and other domestic animals. Silent streams of Yamuna river bordering the place are enchanting with all flowers in full-bloom, many of them floating over the flowing water as if welcoming us with all their grace. The huge mountains on the three sides and the river at their foothills seem to be heartening to Nanda Maharaj and other village lords and relieving their concern for safety of the place.

The river Yamuna is flowing quietly and making a comforting noise with gentle waves as if inviting us into her safe hold. The surrounding flowery gardens with small rivulets in between and some huge and strong trees of all sorts with their long branches hovering in and around, soon became the most sought-after and desirable place on all days for us. It is particularly so for all the boys to rear the large flock of cows and calves and to happily spend their time.

The most relishing fact for all *gopalas* is that Balarama and Krishna have now grown up and are allowed to join them on all errands. The vast stretch of agricultural fields on one side till the foot of the distant hills is available for producing paddy. The many grassy and fully green grounds in between has presented grazing ground for the vast fleet of cows. The beautiful and flowery gardens on the other side strewn with narrow rivulets and with the Yamuna river flowing in a parallel course to these gardens has provided lot of living space for all of us in Brindavan.

My father pointed to me at the huge and mighty mountain silhouetted against the far distant sky and looking majestically and he said to me it is the Govardhana *parvat* or *giri*[105]. To my eyes, it appears to stand just opposite to our new small house. Also, it looks to my young mind as if some holy person is sitting firmly in deep meditation.

It had taken some days for us to settle in the new place making necessary arrangements in each house and especially for protection of the cows and their needs. Nanda maharaj and all other elders were busy with the paddy activities. The *gopala* boys are engaged in their usual job of grazing the cows but they are now more attracted and boisterous towards the work assigned to them because Balarama and Krishna are now with them every day.

105 *parvat* or *giri* means mountain

Just a few days after, all in Brindavan could realize that the sinful and atrocious attacks by *asuras* indeed started to recur. This is against the wishful thinking and earlier belief that they may escape from these unfortunate incidents by change of living place. Whilst this has caused immense disappointment to all, it is followed by a grand transformation in the perception of both young and old towards the young Krishna. In Gokula, all of us entertained the idea that some invisible shakti or divine power had protected the little Krishna from all the unfortunate incidents that took place. The elders in fact had dismissed the information received from some of the *gopala* boys that little Kishna himself had caused the two tall and strong trees to fall by drawing the mortar in between the two. Here in Brindavan, when the *gopala* boys informed and described the elders how Krishna has saved them and the cows on many occasions from the sudden vicious attacks from *asuras*, all had begun to truly grasp the situation. The events as described by the *gopala* boys seem to have taken place in the following fashion.

One *asura*[106] in the shape of a calf secretively entered the herd. How Krishna could identify him they could not decipher. Before they have come out of their fear which suddenly gripped them by the *asura's* appearance so near to them, Balarama has already picked the spurious cow by its legs and killed it and effortlessly thrown it far away from the herd thus bringing an end to the *asura's* life.

On some other day, to their shock, an *asura*[107] in the guise of a huge crane unexpectedly came in their way and grabbed Krishna and eaten him away. Soon after some few moments, they observed that the crane could not bear Krishna inside and has to push him

106 another demon sent by Kamsa
107 bakasura

out of its stomach. Krishna then took hold of its two long beaks and tore them apart like tearing a grass blade into two along its length. The sudden occurrence of event stunned them all but on seeing the miraculous act of Krishna, it brought tremendous joy to the *gopalas.* It is a big relief to the elders also, on hearing the news from the boys after their return. Next followed the death of one more *asura*[108] in the shape of a python in the hands of our beloved Krishna who thus saved the lives of all *gopalas* from the clutches of death. These gory incidents as elaborated by *gopalas* completely surprised Nanda maharaj and all the elders and started convincing them about the mysterious powers possessed by Krishna. In the case of the last *asura*'s death in the hands of Krishna, one aspect has remained as a surprise for all. All came to know about this event from the *gopalas* some one year before. On a recent day, the same *gopala* boys after their return from the days' chores informed again in their houses about the death of the *asura* as if the incident has taken place just this day. This is a [109]mystery that surprised all in Brindavan for some time but,

---

108 aghasura

109 The mystery around the death of *Aghasura* is Lord Krishna's *adbhuta leela* (wonderful divine act). Krishna is of five years old when the *asura* has met his death. It so happened that on one day after an year, the *gopala* boys who returned home with all the cows from their day's work again informed in their houses that Krishna has killed the *aghasura* - an *asura* in the shape of a huge serpent - and saved all of them from the clutches of death. This surprised the king Parishit who was listening with all devotion and with rapt attention to the sweet and exemplary tales of Sri Krishna, the *Paramaatma*'s incarnation in Dwapur yuga in this mortal world. His curiosity thus aroused, Parishit requested Suka Maharshi to enlighten him on this surprising behavior of the *gopala* boys. Suka Maharshi with his yogic power could perceive the reason behind the one year lapse on the part of *gopala* boys. Deriving immense pleasure from the knowledge he got on the sequence of events that lead to such lapse on the part of *gopalas*, he appraised the king

however, they later brushed it aside as a some sort of lapse on the part of these boys.

Capping all these events, there had been some incidents that have left no doubt in the minds of all to strongly believe that Krishna is a God-given gift of Yasoda *tayi* and Nanda maharaj possessing divine powers. It happened before the eyes of all in Brindavan and it has

---

Parishit of the mystery. Suka Maharshi told the king Parishit that it was the handiwork of Brahma, the Lord of creation of this universe,. When Brahma learnt about the superlative powers of Krishna in Brindavan, he wished to test him without knowing that Krishna is the *Paramaatma*'s incarnation in Dwapur yuga with the sole *aim of

*यदा यदा हि धर्मस्य ग्लानिर्भवति भारत।
अभ्युत्थानमधर्मस्य तदात्मानं सृजाम्यहम्॥ Bhagavad Gita, chapter 4 – *Karma yoga*

punishing the wicked and establishing dharma in the world. Soon after Aghasura's death and on the same day, Brahma hid the *gopalas* along with their cattle and made them disappear. Krishna, being *Paramaatma* himself, could grasp the situation and showed his superlative powers by assuming the appearances of all the *gopala* boys and the cattle and returned to their respective homes. Life was same for all the folk in Brindavan without any chance of knowing the truth. At the end of one year which is nothing but a short duration for Brahma on his time scale, he had seen, to his surprise, all the boys and cattle engaged in their activities in Brindavan as in the past, even though the real boys and the cattle are still with him in his hiding place. He could immediately could decipher the reason and without any further delay he appeared before Sri Krishna and offered his apologies for entertaining the idea of testing the *paramaatma* HIMSELF and offered his prayers. On that day, when the real boys and cattle who had been released by Brahma, returned their homes one year after, happened to narrate the incident of their encounter with Aghasura and his death in the hands of Krishna. The one year of their absence, none of them was aware of. Hearing to this *adbhuta leela* or divine episode on manifestation of Sri Krishna, King Parishit was filled with unbounded happiness and paid his prayers to HIM.

brought in a pious transformation in their thinking, speech and action.

There is a pond some distance away from the village where all of us are prohibited to go and fetch water. It seems that it is inhabited by a family of snakes with Kaliya as its head. One day it seems that the *gopalas* are attacked by the poisonous snake. With an intention to subdue the snake, Krishna jumped into the pond in search of the snake. On seeing Krishna getting inside the water, *gopalas* rushed into the village with fear and informed all. Everybody immediately ran towards the pond with all anxiety and to their surprise, Krishna by that time not only tamed the gigantic snake, caught its tail with his bare hands and stationed himself on its large head in a dancing pose[110]. All got bewildered by the sight of the young Krishna standing in the midst of the pond over the Kaliya's hooded head with his favorite peacock feather in his curly hair and playing his *basuri* (flute) so melodiously that a strange feeling of devotion and love befallen on them all. They could recover from their stupefied situation, only when they saw

---

110 The serpent Kaliya was once afraid of Garuda who is the divine eagle and the *vahanam* (mount) of Vishnu, God's incarnate and the serpent was running all over the *bhuvanas* (worlds) for fear of his life. Finally, he took refuge in a lake near the river Yamuna in Brindavan. He was aware that Garuda has been cursed by the *rishi* (sage Saubhari) and prohibited entry into this lake (Chapter 17, canto 10, Maha Bhagavatam of Veda Vyasa. Since then the serpent was residing in this lake with his family but in turn causing much inconvenience and danger to all in Brindavan. Now, having been vanquished, seriously injured and bruised in the fight with Sri Krishna, he has sought HIS *saranu* (shelter) along with the lady serpents. Being a *saranagata vaschala* (Supreme purusha who obliges a devotee's prayer for a relief), Sri Krishna excused Kaliya. He also gave assurance that with the pious imprints of HIS feet on his hood, Garuda no longer does any harm to him and commanded him to leave Brindavan which Kaliya complied with for the delight of all in Brindavan.

Yasoda *tayi* weeping and frantically trying to go near to Krishna in the waters. Nobody had any idea how all of them – young and old – could control their senses on that eventful day. They all brought Krishna back home carrying him on their shoulders with the mixed feelings of surprise and shock and in a state of devotional feeling towards Krishna.

2.3.1 Brindavan enlightened by Divine Krishna

All through the rainy and autumn seasons, Brindavan looked enchanting and beautiful. As if all in nature - cows and calves, all birds including cranes, peacocks and all other beings, animate or inanimate - around are aware of the intimate divine presence of Krishna, the whole place is shining in myriad colors with the rivers being full and flowing serenely and gardens being filled with different flowers fully blossomed and with all reddish pathways bordered on both sides by lush green grassy land. Govardhana *giri* and all other mountains are flourished by the presence of intermingled gorgeous water-falls and by the intermittent hill-tops decorated with thick growth of lush trees on their slopes. While *gopalas* are enjoying the company of Krishna and Balarama all day in the forest along with the cows, *gopikas* are relishing in Krishna's thoughts all time in a day or night. They get so enlivened on hearing Krishna's flute vibrating through the forest, their bodies and minds offer no resistance to their insuppressible desire to resonate with the enchanting sound of the flute[111]. I am familiar to all girls. Only a few of them are elder to me. I am more fond of

111 In Chapter 21, Canto 10 of Srimad-Bhagavatam, sage Veda Vyasa describes in the following *sloka* the enchanting nature of the divine song emanating from the flute:

Radha *didi*[112] who is our immediate neighbor. She is elder to me by a couple of years but she treats me as her own sister and dotes on me like a mother. May be, my deformity – of being dumb by birth – might have made her to take interest in me. From my side, she has made an unfailing imprint in my mind from my younger days. Next to Yasoda *tayi*, I almost adore Radha *didi*. She is my divine and I am her devotee.

One mesmerizing event has occurred that strongly gripped all in Brindavan and indeed helped them to further elevate themselves to lofty heights of divine thinking about Krishna. It is an incident where some ladies have been strangely quizzed by Krishna when they went for their bath in the river. It might have been an embarrassing occasion for them initially but the ladies themselves have realized their fortune in getting enlightened by Krishna about the sublime truth on the reality of this mortal life[113]. They partook the information with all about their transcendental experience. Radha *didi* in a simple and eloquent way made me also know the awe-inspiring truth what Divine Krishna conveyed through HIS

गोप्य: किमाचरदयं कुशलं स्म वेणुर् दामोदराधरसुधामपि गोपिकानाम् । भुंक्ते स्वयं यदवशिष्टरसं ह्रदिन्यो हृष्यत्त्वचोऽश्रु मुमुचुस्तरवो यथार्या: ॥९॥	<u>Meaning:</u> *Gopikas* exclaim in wonder; What severe and what auspicious acts the flute might have performed to drink the nectar of HIS lips leaving only the taste to them. Also, they praise the bamboo trees and the rivers, the forefathers of the flute for their fortune of having begot such a child – the flute - to be adorned on Divine Krishna's hands

112 *didi* means sister

113 The impermanent value of the mortal life is described in the following *sloka* in Bhagavad Gita (Chapter2)

action. I could observe that Radha *didi*, while explaining to me, has herself got bewitched by the impact of what she also learnt through the eventful episode. With all attention of a devotee, I tried to assimilate what all she tried to explain to me. It is all about the basic truth that all beings in this mortal world are, after all, HIS creation. We all, out of our ego and ignorance, feel that what we possess is ours and are caught in the web of many desires and affected by the twin consequences of happiness and sorrow. The divine truth is that one must always try to be free of this possessiveness. When the body is not ours and when the self within everyone is *Paramaatma* HIMSELF, where is 'I' and 'we'! It is all *maya* or delusion that veils every-self from knowing this truth.

All, what Radha *didi* explained to me today, seem to be outwardly simple and clear. But she herself told me that this is the sublime truth what the *rishis* (sages) of the ancient past and the present times are most aspiring to achieve[114]. My divine teacher Radha *didi* did definitely impress my ignorant soul, at least in firmly understanding that my deformity is also *Paramaatma*'s will and so why to worry?.

अव्यक्तादीनि भूतानि व्यक्तमध्यानि भारत। अव्यक्तनिधनान्येव तत्र का परिदेवना॥2.28॥	Meaning of the verse: Beings are not manifest in the beginning and also unmanifest in their end. These bodies are manifest only in the intermediate state and thus its existence is illusory. So, what to grieve about?

114 In Svetasvatara Upanishad, one finds a vivid discussion on this sublime truth. In this context, the following questioning by the disciples is highly significant:

2.3.2 Krishna lifts Govarhana giri and saves all in Brindavan

Before the Kalindi incident began to fade out of our minds, all in Brindavan have encountered yet another mysterious, mesmerizing and incredible happening. It all started with Nanda maharaj and elders planning to perform the yearly *puja* festival – a worshipping festival - to appease the rain gods and specifically Indra, the Lord of heavens. It seems that Krishna advised them instead, to do worship for the pleasure of cows and hills because of which they are all sustained in all seasons and thus suggested to offer prayers to Govardhan *giri*.

Nanda maharaj and the elders agreed for the suggestion and initiated the preparations with all enthusiasm and grand celebration. But, immediately after successful completion of the prayers to Govardhana *giri*, a surprising, unexpected and harmful situation is awaiting them. Without any indication, the weather conditions all around the village are completely spoiled and all are baffled by

---

किं कारणं ब्रह्म कुतः स्म जाता जीवाम केन क्व च सम्प्रतिष्ठा । अधिष्ठिताः केन सुखेतरेषु वर्तामहे ब्रह्मविदो व्यवस्थाम् ॥ १ ॥	<u>Meaning of the verse:</u> They wondered, "whence are we born? why do we live? Where is our final rest? Under whose orders are we? What is the power behind our actions? who commands the law of happiness and misery?". Being rishis themselves, they found the truth (by meditation): - as long as the self does not know that Supreme Power, it gets attached to worldly pleasures and it is bound, but when it knows *Paramaatma,* all fetters, shackles or bondages fall away from the individual self and he gets fixed on *Paramaatma.*

an instant downpour of thunderous rain. Everything turned out to be helter-skelter and chaotic and the whole village soon wore a disastrous look leaving all in dismay and fear. Some elders even surmised and hinted to Nanda maharaj that the rain Gods and their master Indra were dissatisfied with the new decision to worship Govardhan *giri* and being angry with the villagers on this account, they are showing their might in the shape of this havoc. The incessant rains battered all their living conditions causing untold misery to them and more so to the cattle.

Krishna lifting Govardhana giri on HIS little finger

Then, the [115]most extraordinary and unbelievable scene unfolded before their bewildering eyes. It is a sight that stunned and numbed

115 This strange episode is Krishna's another *adbhuta leela.* He wishes to subdue the pride of Indra, the lord of Heavens. Krishna's suggestion to the elders in Brindavan to perform *puja* (worship) to Govardhana *giri* instead of Indra was made to serve this purpose. The subsequent event of Sri Krishna lifting, just by HIS little finger, of Govardhana *giri* and providing shelter and protection to all HIS people is in consonance with *Paramaatma*'s assurance of safety to HIS devotees who worship HIM always with *ananya bhakti*

their minds with disbelief. Krishna with his beautiful countenance and a bewitching smile on his face lifted the whole mighty Govaradhana *giri* on his little finger in such a nonchalant manner that he, standing underneath the *parvat*, looked playful and joyous while the whole and vast expanse underneath opened up a safe place for all to occupy and take shelter along with all the cows and calves. Soon, the earlier all-gloomy and disheartened atmosphere changed into one of jubilation and satisfaction. Balarama, all other boys and elders soon started guiding and leading all our families to be safely placed in the shelter and to settle comfortably. Even though all our minds are finally put to rest and our well-being taken care of by Krishna, the only note of unhappiness for all of us at this mystifying moment is to find Yasoda *tayi* with uncontrollable grief and in utter anxiety about her divine son's well-being. Rohini *tayi* is by her side consoling her all through and Nanda maharaj also comforting her without exposing his own bewilderment and apprehensions about the unexpected turn of events.

It is for full seven days, the village was continuously afflicted by the rains but to our surprise, we found that the rains stopped with the same suddenness as observed when they started a week before.

(utmost devotion) and with *nishkama karma* (selfless action) as enunciated in *sloka* 22 of Chapter 9 in Bhagavad Gita:

अनन्याश्चिन्तयन्तो मां ये जनाः पर्युपासते।
एषां नित्याभियुक्तानां योगक्षेमं वहाम्यहम्॥ 9.22

Witnessing such a *adbhuta leela* by Sri Krishna, Indra repented and came to the realization that Sri Krishna is none other than the *Parama Purusha* (supreme soul) and *Paramaatma* only. He immediately fell on his feet before Sri Krishna and worshipped HIM with all humility and sought *Paramaatma*'s pardon for his hasty and dastardly retribution on people in Brindavan. Bhagawaan Sri Krishna pardoned Indra with the advice to be always sober and without pride.

Anyhow, with scant attention towards the situation outside, all of us have enjoyed the new found comfort under the protection given by Krishna. Also, all what happened and what we experienced all through the last few memorable days brought in a remarkable transformation in the thinking of almost all in Brindavan. It is now a fact that the elders including Nanda maharaj have now been in a trance with the greatest feeling of elation that they are all bestowed by the grace of the Divine Krishna and they now entertain the firm belief that Krishna is none other than God incarnate.

I heard my father telling my mother with a voice choked with emotion about the discussions all the elders had with Nanda maharaj after this memorable incident. All came to same agreement that a young lad lifting Govardhana *giri* and even subduing a gigantic venomous snake Kaliya is not a task possible to an ordinary mortal. This is further corroborated by Nanda maharaj himself who remembered and shared the purport of his discussions he had with Garg mahamuni[116] long time back in the past. The *mahamuni*, it seems, told him that Krishna is indeed Srimannarayana's or *Paramaatma*'s incarnation in this *Dwapur yuga* with the divine resolve of punishing the wicked and safeguard *dharma* on this earth[117]. With this revelation from Nanda maharaj, all in Brindavan are gripped by a wonderful feeling of elation and wondered what multitude of good

116 Garg mahamuni is the family priest of the yadu-vamsa (Yadu family); he performed the name-giving ceremony for Kṛiṣhṇa and Balarama in a solitary place so as to keep it unknown to the cruel king Kamsa.

117 Here, one must remember what Bhagawaan Sri Krishna has said in the following *sloka* 8 of chapter 4 in Bhagavad Gita:

परित्राणाय साधूनां विनाशाय च दुष्कृताम् । धर्मसंस्थापनार्थाय सम्भवामि युगे युगे ॥ 4.8 ॥	Meaning: Whenever there is a decline of dharma (righteousness), and rise of adharma (unrighteousness), then I incarnate myself

deeds they all might have done in their previous births to deserve this fortune of being under *Paramaatma*'s protection and enjoying HIS sublime proximity! This is just the thought rejoicing the minds of all. When I heard my aged father trying to explain the gist of this discussion, it looked for me standing in the cowshed, that the cows in our courtyard also are in rapt attention as if they also could grasp what is being talked about.

2.4 Devotees in Brindavan and Divine Krishna

Of late, for almost everyone - young and old -, life changed in Brindavan. There is a new found enthusiasm coupled with a strange feeling of some amazement lingering in their minds. My ignorant mind also could decipher the reason. This must be because during the last event of Govardhana *giri puja*, they were all direct witnesses to the divinely omnipotence of Krishna. They have got enlightened enough in this respect that for them, *Paramaatma* is before them in the divine form of Krishna. This realization filled their hearts with contentment. For these elderly people including my parents, Krishna has entered into their daily routine of worshiping. Most of them directed their *puja* (worship) towards Krishna by their actions and thoughts. I also heard my parents discussing about the frequent meetings of the village elders in Nanda maharaj's house and their talks always centering on Krishna and Krishna only. That certain elders not having the same opinion as of all others is also perceived. They, it seems, are not in agreement[118] with others as regards the divine nature of Krishna.

As for Yasoda *tayi*, she is deeply caught in between her motherly love and affection towards Krishna and the grand revelation that

118 Bhagawaan Sri Krishna himself has conveyed in the following *sloka 11* of Chapter 9 of Bhagavad Gita:

her young lad is indeed an incarnation of *Paramaatma* and she is the mother of the omnipresent, omniscient and omnipresent[119] *Paramaatma*. In caressing HIM and even while doing all the necessary chores for HIM, she has now transformed into a beloved devotee rather than a doting mother. She is fully engaged in the service of her divine Krishna both outwardly and inwardly – both in action and thought. However, one can imagine that being now aware of the fact that she is only HIS foster mother and knowing the supreme truth underlying HIS incarnation in Madhura, she may also be in a state of perpetual anxiety that HE may leave for Madhura in near future.

The behavior and movements of other ladies also is not different. Both their minds and looks also are rivetted on HIM and on HIS prayers as if they are doing penance for their earlier complaining attitude on Krishna's pranks in their houses. The whole Brindavan has become *Paramaatma*'s abode and how much superlative blessing it is for all living in the divine vicinity of *Paramaatma!*

अवजानन्ति मां मूढा मानुषीं तनुमाश्रितम् । परं भावमजानन्तो मम भूतमहेश्वरम् ॥ 9.11 ॥	Meaning: Since I incarnate in human form, some ignorant souls, being unaware of my all-pervading nature, show no regard for me

119 The following *sloka* of Chapter 8 in Bhagavad Gita describes *Paramaatma*:

अधिभूतं क्षरो भावः पुरुषश्चाधिदैवतम्। अधियज्ञोऽहमेवात्र देहे देहभृतां वर॥8.4॥	Meaning of the verse: Paramaatma is *Adhibhoota* - that which underlies all perishable elements; HE is *Adhidaivata* - that which underlies all the dieties and HE is *Adhiyajna* – that who sustains all *yajnaas* (actions)

2.4.1 *Gopala* boys and *gopika* girls and Divine Krishna

All girls and boys in Brindavan are now more devoted to Krishna. Their earlier playful intimacy towards little Krishna in Gokula transformed to pure devotion - a sublime feeling of a devotee towards the Divine. Their minds and hearts are throbbing for HIS presence always. All their thoughts are routed towards HIM day-in and day-out. Their love which they earlier had towards Krishna has now taken the shape of pure devotion. The boys, in particular, are feeling anxious every day and looking for their day-time errand with great expectations so that they can be in the close company of Krishna. Even after their return to their homes, they are in a constant remembrance of HIM and especially engage themselves in explaining their parents about how they have spent their time with the beloved Krishna in the forests.

For the *gopikas*, the change in their behavior towards Krishna is more significant and transparent. For them Krishna is their Divine. Krishna is now the idol for all the girls – unmarried and married. For the elders, Krishna is the supreme *Paramaatma* and HE is the final abode[120]. For the girls, HE is the supreme and divine lover. Radha *didi* is no exception and in fact, to my little observatory mind, she looks that she got more captivated by Krishna and devoutly devoted to HIM. In recent times, my wanderings with her became few and far between. My Divine lady seems to forsake me in search of her Divine. She must be dearer to Krishna also and the others may even be a little envious of her in this respect. This may be, however, a poor conjecture on my part because they are intimately affectionate towards each other.

2.4.2 Radha, the devotee and Divine Krishna

For Radha *didi* and all *gopikas*, Brindavan is the heaven with Krishna only as their Lord. The nearby flowery gardens and the shiny and vast sand bed of the river Yamuna accompanied by its tranquil flow of water are their divine habitats in the night hours and often have become meeting places to enjoy their Lord's celestial presence. For

---

120

हे गोपालक! हे कृपाजलनिधे! हे सिन्धुकन्यपते! हे कम्सान्तक! हे गजेन्द्र करुणा पारीण! हे माधव। हे रामानुज! हे जगत्रय गुरो! हे पुन्डरीकाक्ष! माम् हे गोपीजननाथ! पालय परम् जानामि न त्वम् विना। This is the verse 21 in Mukundamala *stotram* (prayer) of saintly king Kulasekhara Alwar of century. Mukunadamala meaning a garland of hymns, is a composition in Sanskrit scented with intense *bhakti* towards Lord Krishna. It consists of around 40 verses with such a devotional depth that raised the composition to the crest of the Bhakti movement in India.	Essential meaning of the verse: The Lord is the ocean of compassion, the destroyer of Kamsa and has, in fact, saved in the past, many *jivas* (beings) like Gajendra (of Gajendra moksha in Canto 8, Veda Vyasa's Maha Bhagavatam). HE is the Viswa guru and the Lord of the Gopis of Brindavan. O the Supreme Protector! bless me, O Lord! I know no one else other than YOU

them, everything that belongs to the Lord is beautiful[121]. Bewitched by the Divine presence of Krishna, the *gopikas* have entirely surrendered themselves to HIM as true devotees. At times, I also

---

121 The words 'beauty' and 'beautiful' are part of *Paramaatma*'s creation and it is no surprise that HE must be beautiful. A composition namely मधुराष्टकम् (Madhurashtakam) written by Sri Vallabhacharya in sanskrit speaks of *Paramaatma*'s beauty so enchantingly and soul-searchingly that any one is struck by its *madhuryam* (sweetness) in every verse. Sri Vallabhacharya is a saint and philosopher of 15th century who originally belongs to Andhra region in South India. He established his philosophy of Pushti Marga, i.e., the Path of Grace in North India and according to which a devotee sees only Sri Krishna and none other than Lord Krishna everywhere. This composition Madhurashtakam consists of 8 devotional verses and it is a pinnacle of *bhakti* (devotion) towards Lord Krishna. All the eight verses are replete or filled with full of love and devotion to Krishna in the form of a transcendental or divine singing by a devotee. The devotee sings as if the Lord is before him and as if he is in a trance attracted by the beauty of Bhagawaan Sri Krishna in everything that belongs to the Lord – the beautiful face, the beautiful lips, the beautiful eyes, the beautiful smile, the Lord's beautiful stride. For the devotee, even the Lord's *murali* (flute) is beautiful, the lord's hands and the Lord's legs are beautiful and Lord's every *anuvu* (atom) is beautiful in the devotee's mind. The eight verses are:

अधरं मधुरं वदनं मधुरं
नयनं मधुरं हसितं मधुरम् ।
हृदयं मधुरं गमनं मधुरं
मधुराधिपतेरखिलं मधुरम् ॥ 1 ॥

वचनं मधुरं चरितं मधुरं
वसनं मधुरं वलितं मधुरं ।
चलितं मधुरं भ्रमितं मधुरं
मधुराधिपतेरखिलं मधुरम् ॥ 2 ॥

वेणु-र्मधुरो रेणु-र्मधुरः
पाणि-र्मधुरः पादौ मधुरौ ।
नृत्यं मधुरं सख्यं मधुरं
मधुराधिपतेरखिलं मधुरम् ॥ 3 ॥

गीतं मधुरं पीतं मधुरं
भुक्तं मधुरं सुप्तं मधुरं ।
रूपं मधुरं तिलकं मधुरं
मधुराधिपतेरखिलं मधुरम् ॥ 4 ॥

करणं मधुरं तरणं मधुरं
हरणं मधुरं स्मरणं मधुरं ।
वमितं मधुरं शमितं मधुरं
मधुराधिपतेरखिलं मधुरम् ॥ 5 ॥

गुञ्जा मधुरा माला मधुरा
यमुना मधुरा वीची मधुरा ।
सलिलं मधुरं कमलं मधुरं
मधुराधिपतेरखिलं मधुरम् ॥ 6 ॥

गोपी मधुरा लीला मधुरा
युक्तं मधुरं मुक्तं मधुरं ।
दृष्टं मधुरं शिष्टं मधुरं
मधुराधिपतेरखिलं मधुरम् ॥ 7 ॥

गोपा मधुरा गावो मधुरा
यष्टि र्मधुरा सृष्टि र्मधुरा ।
दलितं मधुरं फलितं मधुरं
मधुराधिपतेरखिलं मधुरम् ॥ 8 ॥

Here it is also apt and appropriate to remind ourselves of Leelasuka's Krishna Karnamritam. Leelasuka's original name is Bilavamangala (of 13th century and from Kerala state, India). He acquired the name Leelasuka because of his becoming immersed in the *leela* (feat/deed) of Krishna and describing it in detail like Suka maharshi who recited and explained Bhagavatam to king Parishit. In the following *sloka* of Krishna Karnamritam, Leelasuka describes HIM in an alluring way:

acted as a reliable messenger between them to exchange messages. Even though they have absolute faith on each other, there are occasions when, blinded by their devotion to Krishna, most of the *gopikas* had suspicion on specifically about Radha *didi* whether she has scored over them in wooing HIM towards herself. Radha *didi* once explained to me that on one night when the *gopikas* are fully absorbed in relishing Divine Krishna's proximity so near to them and are filled with the pride of having Krishna's undivided attention towards them, HE made HIMSELF invisible leaving the *gopikas* in utter despair and disappointment. They have made frantic search[122] in all their familiar places for their beloved God. Finding later a pair

---

मधुरं मधुरं वपु रस्य विभो- र्मधुरं मधुरं वदनं मधुरम् । मधुगन्धि मृदुस्मित मेत दहो मधुरं मधुरं मधुरं मधुरम् ॥ ९१ ॥	Meaning: Everything with reference to the Lord is sweet, because He himself is sweet. His face, the fragrance on Him and His smile, everything is sweet, sweet *nothing but sweet.* In MadhurashTakam also, we have the line '*madhuradhipater-akhilam madhuram'* and the same idea is reflected here in this sloka.

122 Veda Vyasa in describing the profound sorrow of the *gopikas* in chapter 30, canto 10 of Maha Bhagavatam, expressed in a subtle way, *Paramaatma's* integral divinity and HIS omnipresence through the following *slokas* -it is indeed the purport contained in each and every *sloka* of Maha Bhagavatam):

दृष्टो वः कच्चिदश्वत्थ प्लक्ष न्यग्रोध नो मनः नन्दसूनुर्गतो हृत्वा प्रेमहासावलोकनैः	Meaning: The *gopikas* are asking *asvattha* (fig) and *nyagrodha* (banyan) trees if they have seen Krishna who is the son of Nanda maharaj and who has gone away after stealing their minds with HIS loving smiles and glances.

of footsteps[123] before them on the path and following them further, they had the suspicion that their Lord has already been with none other than Radha *didi* in some other secluded place. It further accentuated their pangs of jealousy when they have found a few paces after, thick marks of a single foot prints. Probably their Divine Krishna was possibly carrying HIS companion in HIS hands. But,

मालत्यदर्शि वः कच्चिन् मल्लिके जातियूथिके प्रीतिं वो जनयन् यातः करस्पर्शेन माधवः	<u>Meaning:</u> When they had no reply from the trees, the *gopikas* question the different jasmine flowers whether Divine Krishna has gone by their side. Because, they thought that HE definitely might have given immense pleasure to them with the touch of HIS hand.
किं ते कृतं क्षिति तपो बत केशवाङ्घ्रि- स्पर्शोत्सवोत्पुलकिताङ्गरुहैर्विभासि अप्यङ्घ्रिसम्भव उरुक्रमविक्रमाद्वा आहो वराहवपुषः परिरम्भणेन	<u>Meaning:</u> The *gopikas* even asked the mother earth if she had seen Lord Krishna passing by her side. They observed that the mother earth appeared beautiful and it must be because of the touch of the beautiful feet of Lord Krishna. They also exclaimed whether that grandeur was of earlier touch by the Lord during HIS incarnations as Vamana or Varaha.

123 It is indeed interesting and also amusing to note *gopikas* even in their current condition of extreme grief, exhibiting their alertness in drawing sensible conclusions from the footprints they observed on the pathway lighted by moonlight. This, one finds in the following *slokas* in Chapter 30, canto 10 of Maha Bhagavatam by Veda Vyasa.

कस्याः पदानि चैतानि याताया नन्दसूनुना अंसन्यस्तप्रकोष्ठायाः करेणोः करिणा यथा	<u>Meaning:</u> Here we see the footprints of some *gopika* who must have been walking along with the son of Nanda maharaja

to their added surprise, they sighted Radha *didi* alone in the forest deserted by their beloved Lord.

Here, Radha *didi*, with all her intense devotion to the Lord springing from her looks, explained to me, an ignorant soul, that one should be a devout devotee of *Paramaatma* to be eligible for HIS grace. Pure devotion and total surrender only tie *Paramaatma* to a worshipper. The *gopikas*, having been mellowed down by their remorse and having been cleansed of their proud attitude, they began pouring out their prayers in right earnest with a request for a union with their Lord. Radha *didi* delightfully narrated to me how Divine

---

इमान्यधिकमग्नानि पदानि वहतो वधूम् गोप्य: पश्यत कृष्णस्य भाराक्रान्तस्य कामिन: अत्रावरोपिता कान्ता पुष्पहेतोर्महात्मना	<u>Meaning:</u> They observed in one place deep impressions of footprints and they conjectured that Krishna was carrying the weight of His beloved *gopika* and it must have been difficult for Him. And over here that intelligent boy must have put Her down to gather some flowers
अत्र प्रसूनावचय: प्रियार्थे प्रेयसा कृत: प्रपदाक्रमण एते पश्यतासकले पदे	<u>Meaning:</u> In another place, they observed the impression of only the front part the feet. They imagined that their beloved Krishna was standing on His toes to reach flowers and collect them for HIS dear *gopika*.

Krishna reappeared before them and comforted them[124] with HIS transcendental and caring glances.

124 The *gopikas*, thus reunited with their Divine Krishna, forgot their distress due to the just concluded separation from HIM. The following *sloka* in chapter 33, canto 10 of Maha Bhagavatam of Veda Vyasa, describes the divine *rasa kreeda* (celestial dance):

योगेश्वरेण कृष्णेन तासां मध्ये द्वयोर्द्वयोः प्रविष्टेन गृहीतानां कण्ठे स्वनिकटं स्त्रियः	<u>Meaning:</u> Lord Krishna pleased the *gopikas* and the whole universe with the enchanting *rasa kreeda*. With the *gopikas* in a circle around HIM, Lord Krishna presented HIMSELF between each pair of *gopikas* and impressed all of them with the feeling that He was standing next to each one of them

In a very scintillating way, Leela Suka in his Krishna Karnamritam, describes the *Rasa kreeda* in this following sloka:

अङ्गना मङ्गना मन्तरे माधवो माधवं माधवं चान्तरे णाङ्गना । इत्थ माकल्पिते मण्डले मध्यगः सञ्जगौ वेणुना देवकीनन्दनः ॥ ३५ ॥	<u>Meaning:</u> Krishna appears HIMSELF in many forms and dances with the *gopikas.* HE stands in between two *gopikas* and thus each *gopika* in-between two forms of the Divine Krishna. In the middle of the circle thus formed, Krishna was playing HIS flute. The eight *slokas* beginning with this one, describe the *rasa kreeda* This has a philosophical significance. The *gopikas* are the *jivas,* each one of them having the Lord as the inner self. Also, HE is the supreme self. Thus, the world is the *rasa kreeda* of the Lord. When the *jiva* joins hands with the Lord, it gives *ateendriya bliss* (immeasurable joy).

Krishna and *gopikas* in *rasa kreeda*

2.5 Akrura, the devotee and journey of Divine Krishna to Madhura

All in Brindavan are so glued to their new way of life devoted to Divine Krishna that the slaying by HIM of Aristasura and also the *asuras* Kesi and Vyoma had least perturbed them. But, on one day, when the news reached all of them that a brahmin Akrura arrived in Brindavan to take Krishna and Balarama to Madhura, it had shaken them like a thunderbolt. Everyone could easily understand that it was only at the behest of the wicked and fierce king Kamsa, Akrura's visit was planned to take away their Divine Krishna. Very well knowing by now that the present proposal to bring them to his court also must be a vicious plot of the king to do harm to the beloved Krishna and Balarama, all of them soon made an attempt to impress Nanda maharaj to realize the king's cruel plot and to dissuade him to accept for their journey to Madhura. Nanda maharaj however assuaged their fear by reminding them of the Divine power of the two boys and by assuring them that everything would culminate according to the pre-destined celestial order of happening of events and none could do harm to the boys.

The impending departure of Divine Krishna left everyone in Brindavan without any exception in a state of indescribable agony. The boys were unable to understand the reason why their Divine mate had to leave them and why HE did not as well express HIS refusal to follow Akrura to Madhura.

For the girls, it was an unbearable situation and they wer unable to compromise for the miserable scenario of Krishna leaving them and proceeding to Madhura. They were so caustic of HIM that, in their deep sorrow, they started wailing and accusing HIM of intentionally departing to the more attractive and alluring Madhura. They were even blaming Akrura for causing the separation of their Lord from them, even though they came to know that Akrura is a devout devotee of Divine Krishna and his devotion to Krishna is as pristine as theirs. We all in Brindavan came to know from some of the *gopala* boys that the brahmin, soon after entering the premises of Brindavan alighted from his chariot and, to their surprise and disbelief, began rolling on the muddy pathway and exhibiting strange behavior[125]. On being informed of this news, Nanda maharaj explained to all elders that Akrura is such a pure and pious brahmin and accepted the errand

125 Akrura, from the instant he started in Madura on the way to Brindavan, is all excited about his blissful meeting with Lord Krishna in Brindavan. He is even grateful to the wicked king Kamsa to be given this errand even though he is aware of the evil intention of the king behind the injunction. In the following *slokas*, sage Veda Vyasa vividly describes the pious qualities of this brahmin:

from Kamsa, only to pay his salutations to Krishna, fully knowing the divine intentions of HIS incarnation in this yuga.

But, whatever good tidings the future might bring in, because of the two brothers visiting Madura, *gopikas* could not compromise with the prospects of Krishna leaving them. As I could easily decipher, they had gone into a frenzy of untold sorrow. It was as if their vital airs were drawn out of them and were being transported elsewhere. Their agony made them numb with their unbounded grief and they became oblivious of all their external senses[126]. Remembering their Divine's charming smiles and caressing embraces, their minds were

---

ममाद्यामङ्गलं नष्टं फलवांश्चैव मे भवः यन्नमस्ये भगवतो योगिध्येयान्घ्रिपङ्कजम्	Meaning of the verse: Akrura excitedly felt that today his life got fulfilled with all his sins destroyed and he would offer his obeisances to Divine Krishna's lotus feet which is the aspiration of all yogis in meditation
तद्दर्शनाह्लादविवृद्धसम्भ्रमः प्रेम्णोर्ध्वरोमाश्रुकलाकुलेक्षणः रथादवस्कन्द्य स तेष्वचेष्टत प्रभोरमून्यङ्घ्रिरजांस्यहो इति	Meaning of the verse: Seeing Divine krishna's footprints on the pathway, Akrura has got excited with the hair on his body standing erect and with tears rolling down from his eyes. He jumped down from his chariot in ecstasy and began rolling on the footprints of Krishna exclaiming that that is the dust from HIS Feet.

126 Sage Veda Vyasa described the deplorable state of the *gopikas* in the following *slokas* (chapter 39, canto 10 of Maha Bhagavatam. The sage, akin to his style of narration, interspersed with sublime truths of this mortal life as can be deciphered from the *slokas*:

अन्याश्च तदनुध्यान निवृत्ताशेषवृत्तयः नाभ्यजानन्निमं लोकम् आत्मलोकं गता इव	Meaning: *Gopikas* entirely stopped their sensory activities and became fixed in meditation on Krishna. They lost all awareness of the external world, just like *those who attain the state of self-realization.*

wholly engrossed in HIS thoughts, HIS captivating flute-voice and HIS divine acts. This made them lament more over their beloved Krishna's uncaring and hard-hearted behavior for their anguish and distress. They even blamed *Vidhata* (Providence) and Akrura also for creating separation from their Divine Krishna. Their grief knew no bounds when the chariot carrying Balarama and Krishna started moving forward and even when their Divine Krishna tried to pacify them through HIS glances and with an assurance that HE would return.

Divine Krishna as envisioned by gopikas, the devotees and as engrossed in their thoughts while HE leaves for Madhura

एवं ब्रुवाणा विरहातुरा भृशं व्रजस्त्रियः कृष्णविषक्तमानसाः विसृज्य लज्जां रुरुदुः स्म सुस्वरं गोविन्द दामोदर माधवेति	After speaking these words, the ladies of Brindavan, who were so attached to Krishna, felt extremely agitated by their imminent separation from HIM. They forgot all shame and loudly cried out, "O Govinda! O Daamodara! O Maadhava!"

The following sloka in Chapter 39, canto 10, Maha Bhagavatam of Veda Vyasa describes that:

यावदालक्ष्यते केतुर्
यावद्रेणू रथस्य च
अनुप्रस्थापितात्मानो
लेख्यानीवोपलक्षिताः

"With their minds travelling with Divine Krishna, the gopikas are transfixed to the ground like figures in a painting. They stood motionless as long as the flag on the chariot and the dust from the chariot wheels are no longer visible"

[127]*A trivial addendum to this Second Part*

In the days that followed, I, *Achala*, a deformed girl in Brindavan, am fortunate enough to closely follow my divine *didi* Radha in all her moments of sorrow and despondency. She also equally longed for my company; I suppose. It has become my pastime to adore her and follow her in days and nights like a true devotee. I am satisfied with this short life remaining as a devoted deputy to my Divine *didi*. My good old parents are no more and *didi* herself is my mother, father and everything[128]. I consider my life also as one of fulfilment, may be on a minor/insignificant scale. Having been

127 Here, the *gopika Achala* is a fictitious character and is pronounced to be a deformed lady. Let us envision that she was at least fortunate enough to be a living being along with the other more fortunate *gopikas* in Brindavan in Dwapur yuga.

128 For a devotee, the divine is everything. He tries to feel HIS warmth as close as possible like his mother and father, always breath HIM and live with HIM. *Paramaatma* HIMSELF says in *Bhagavad Gita* (*sloka* 17 of Chapter 9):

afflicted by the deformity of being dumb by birth, I may be unable to offer prayers fully, but this is not at all a limitation for me in being devoted to my Divine *didi* through *manasica puja* (worship by thoughts).

पिताहमस्य जगतो माता धाता पितामहः। वेद्यं पवित्रमोङ्कार ऋक्साम यजुरेव च॥9.17॥	Meaning: I am the father of this universe – the mother, the sustainer, the grandfather, the purifier, the knowable, the sacred mono-syllable OM and also the Rig, Sama and the Yajur Vedas

(This *sloka* with meaning as given in the footnote 92 is intentionally repeated here)

Epilogue

The book consists of two parts. As readers might find, out of the narration in the two parts, one belongs to the period of Ramayana in Treta yuga and the other to one related to Krishna *Leela* in Dwapur yuga. The two narrations which are brief and short and which belong to periods separated by many thousands of years are encapsulated in the same book. It is imperative that it is the underlying theme that binds the two narrations. What is the theme ? It is the *devotion* that a worshipper develops towards the supreme architect of this creation, the Divine. It is an unwavering and unflinching faith in HIM that leads one to the path of devotion. This in turn requires a state of mind (to be cultivated) to appreciate HIS creation that surrounds us and to perceive HIM in all beings. Towards this, one needs to rightly utilize this birth in human from[129] which by itself is difficult to get, even though it is impermanent and is riddled with tribulations. Here, we need to carefully assimilate the message contained in the following *sloka* of Bhagavad Gita:

129 In the following *sloka* 33, chapter 9 of Bhagavad Gita, Bhagawaan Sri Krishna conveyed that:

किं पुनर्ब्राह्मणाः पुण्या भक्ता राजर्षयस्तथा । अनित्यमसुखं लोकमिमं प्राप्य भजस्व माम् ॥ 9.33 ॥	Essential meaning of the verse: Having come to this *anityam* (ephemeral or ever changeful); and *asukham* (miserable or unhappy) human world and having attained this human life ***which is a means to liberation,*** be devoted yourself to Me.

संन्यासः कर्मयोगश्च निःश्रेयसकरावुभौ ।
तयोस्तु कर्मसंन्यासात्कर्मयोगो विशिष्यते ॥ 5.2 ॥

In this *sloka*, Bhagawaan Sri Krishna reveals that renunciation of action (by Sankhya *yogi*) and Yoga of action (by Karma *yogi*) both lead to the same goal – self-realization or liberation; but of the two, performance of action is superior to the renunciation of action. The message is a great reliever for common mortals like us. Because, while being a simple house holder and getting engaged in duties and responsibilities, one can as well be a Sankhya *yogi* within our own dwellings by performing actions in the form of *nishkama karma* (action performed with no expectation on the end result). This is to be accompanied by practice of *dhyana* (meditation) to have control over the mind and *indriyas* (sense organs). In addition to having a meditative mind, Bhagawaan Sri Krishna also advocated for us to develop *bhakti* (devotion) towards HIM.

About these vital attributes of a worshipper – meditation and devotion - we find in the following *slokas* of Bhagavad Gita:

For devotion – *sloka* 28, chater 5 of Bhagavad Gita:

यतेन्द्रियमनोबुद्धिर्मुनिर्मोक्षपरायणः ।
विगतेच्छाभयक्रोधो यः सदा मुक्त एव सः ॥ 5.28 ॥

Meaning of the verse: With the mind, senses and intellect controlled, such a man of meditation is freed from desire, fear and anger and is verily liberated for ever.

For Bhakti - *sloka* 47, chater 6 of Bhagavad Gita:

योगिनामपि सर्वेषां मद्गतेनान्तरात्मना ।
श्रद्धावान्भजते यो मां स मे युक्ततमो मतः ॥ 6.47 ॥

Meaning of the verse: Among all the *yogis*, the one who worships HIM with *ananya bhakti* (unflinching devotion) is the most closely united with HIM.

Thus, Bhagawaan is urging us and encouraging us to develop *bhakti* (devotion) and to stay connected with HIM with a steady and firm faith. Such devotees with *acahanchala bhakti* (unwavering or resolute or steadfast devotion) towards *Paramaatma,* one finds with awe and admiration in Sita devi, Anjaneya, Yasoda, Radha and the *gopikas* of Brindavan.

As we must have comprehended from the two parts of the narration in this book, it is an absolute necessity for a devotee to shed the qualities of ego and pride. Sri Krishna, in lifting Govardhana *giri* and providing relief to all in Brindavan is only to subdue Indra, the Lord of Heaven as we understand from the following *sloka* (Maha Bhagavatam of Veda Vyasa):

गम्यतां शक्र भद्रं वः
क्रियतां मेऽनुशासनम्
स्थीयतां स्वाधिकारेषु
युक्तैर्वः स्तम्भवर्जितैः

Meaning of the verse: Indra, you may now go and remain in your appointed position as King of heaven. But be sober without false pride

Similarly, even though *gopikas* know that Krishna is indeed the indweller in the hearts of all embodied souls in this universe, they became proud of their intimacy with HIM and each of them thought that she is the special woman wooed by HIM. The following *sloka* in Maha Bhagavatam of Veda Vyasa stands for their folly in entertaining such a false pride:

तासां तत्सौभगमदं
वीक्ष्य मानं च केशवः
प्रशमाय प्रसादाय
तत्रैवान्तरधीयत

Meaning of the verse: Divine Krishna, seeing the *gopikas* too proud of their good fortune and wishing to relieve them of this pride, soon disappeared from their presence

Even Radha who considered herself the fortunate woman to have received special attention from Divine Krishna faced the same fate by being left by HIM. Tormented by their separation from Krishna, the *gopikas* and Radha, fully absorbed in the thoughts of HIM, became so distraught that they began to sing HIS glories in utter helplessness and wept loudly through the long night in the forest when Divine Krishna reappeared before them. It is a real soul-awakening for all of us to receive the profound message along with the *gopikas* from Divine Krishna through the following *sloka* of Maha Bhagavatam of Veda Vyasa:

नाहं तु सख्यो भजतोऽपि जन्तून्
भजाम्यमीषामनुवृत्तिवृत्तये
यथाधनो लब्धधने विनष्टे
तच्चिन्तयान्यन्निभृतो न वेद

Meaning of the verse: O *gopikas,* the reason I do not immediately respond to the love of living beings even when they worship ME, is that I want to deepen their devotion. It is like a poor man who after gaining some wealth and then losing it becomes so anxious about it that he can think of nothing else.

With these closing words, I sincerely expect that this short narration or a soliloquy of mine on this sublime topic *'Devotion and Divinity'* may be pleasant to those commoners (young and old) like me who have hardly any knowledge about sastras[130] but have unflinching faith in the invisible and all-pervading God almighty. If any of my viewpoints penned in this short narration is incorrect or mis-interpreted by me, I apologize for the same and state that it is only due to my ignorance and limitation of being a commoner.

Many words of *Sanskrit* and *Telugu* languages are retained (and written in italics) in the text to retain some originality and for sake

130 *sastras – Vedas, Upanishads and holy scriptures*

of preciseness. This has become unavoidable and is followed to convey an apt and succinct meaning to the specific verses therein. Readers may find some burden due to this reason and in this respect, I request from the readers for an extra dose of patience and resilience while going through the narration. Meaning of these words in English are of course provided within brackets wherever required. The distinctive feature of the narration is that footnotes (some of which may be too long) convey substantive meaning along with the material in the main text. Also, the footnotes carry more of divine truths to our enlightenment and realization.

In penning my viewpoints during the narrations, I was immensely assisted by reading of books like Srimad Ramayana by Maharshi Valmiki, Srimad Bhagavatam by Veda Vyasa, Srimad Bhagavatam – English translation by Bhaktivedanta Swami Prabhupada, Srimad Bhagavad Gita - Tattvavivecani, Gita press, Gorakhpur, India, Simad Bhagavad Gita – English translation by Swami Gambhirananda.

For meaning of some *slokas* in Bhagavad Gita, I also referred to my earlier book "Bhagavad Gita – my (a commoner's) viewpoint" (published by Notion Press, Chennai, India).

Om Tat Sat

My (a commoner's) passionate entreaty to *Paramaatma*

O *Paramaatma*, for your kindness and favor,
I am eligible or not, I know least; instead,
with tears filling my eyes I request thee
to bestow on me a life in any form on this mother earth,
may be, in the form of a cow, *vanara*, or even a rabbit,
I need to spend a few months in darkness though.
With your light touch, grace me a mind to worship thee only.
I care not for the outside but only yearn to bare my inside.
Let me focus wholly on you only,
my all, only at your shining feet in gratitude.

I salute my loving deity Anjaneya

मनोजवं मारुततुल्यवेगं

जितेन्द्रियं बुद्धिमतां वरिष्ठ।

वातात्मजं वानरयूथमुख्यं

श्रीरामदूतं शरणं प्रपद्ये

Meaning of the verse:

I salute my ideal deity Anjaneya who is swift as the mind and fast as the wind, who is the master of the senses, who is known for his exceptional intelligence, learning and wisdom and who is the son of the wind God and chief among the *vanaras*. From that messenger of Sri Rama, the God incarnate, I seek for refuge by prostrating before him.

www.ingramcontent.com/pod-product-compliance
Lightning Source LLC
LaVergne TN
LVHW091112150826
845673LV00002B/795

* 9 7 9 8 8 9 2 3 3 9 8 1 0 *